THE PROMISE

Also by
ROBERT WESTALL

Blitzcat
Ghost Abbey

THE PROMISE

ROBERT WESTALL

SCHOLASTIC HARDCOVER

Scholastic Inc.
New York

For
Rei Uemura and Mizuhito Kanehara
My friends in Japan

This book was first published in England by Macmillan Publishers, Ltd.
Copyright © 1990 by Robert Westall.
All rights reserved. Published by Scholastic Inc.,
730 Broadway, New York, NY 10003,
by arrangement with Macmillan Children's Books,
a division of Macmillan Publishers Ltd. London and Basingstoke.
SCHOLASTIC HARDCOVER is a registered trademark of Scholastic Inc.

Library of Congress Cataloging-in-Publication Data

Westall, Robert,
The promise/Robert Westall.
p.   cm.
Summary: After his sort-of-girlfriend dies, teen-aged Bob is shocked to discover that their love was stronger than he thought, even strong enough to transcend death.

ISBN 0-590-43760-7

[1. Love — Fiction.   2. Death — Fiction.]   I. Title.
PZ7.W51953Pr   1991
[Fic] — dc20
90-40564
CIP
AC

12 11 10 9 8 7 6 5 4 3 2 1   1 2 3 4 5 6/9

Printed in the U.S.A.   37

First Scholastic printing, March 1991

Chapter One

When I was a lad, before I met Valerie, nothing ever seemed to die.

My Dad would look up from the local paper sometimes, with a sad or pale face. But he wouldn't say, 'Jack Smith's dead.' He'd say, 'I see poor Jack Smith's gotten away.' And I would have a vision of Jack Smith on the run, like an escaped convict in a movie, maybe in rags, but definitely heading for somewhere better. To that eternal life the vicar went on about endlessly in church, three times every Sunday, perhaps . . .

I only ever saw two dead creatures. On a day out to a lighthouse up the Northumbrian coast, I saw a dead seagull; a pretty little thing, a kittiwake I think. Somebody had made a nest for it, from seaweed on a ledge in the cliff. Its eyes were shut, but every soft feather was in place. I stroked them.

'It just looks asleep,' said my mother.

'It'll get a good rest now,' said my Dad.

The whole place seemed filled with love.

The other dead thing was the ginger cat in Billing's Mill. Billing's Mill dominated our skyline, up on its hill; all its sails gone, a squat empty milk-bottle of blackened stone. A sort of castle keep, in which the tom-cat's body lay, a thing of terror and challenge

1

to every boy in the district. You went alone to see it. You approached it, the flies rose in swarms. You looked into the black fathomless sockets where the eyes had been, and then you walked quickly and stiff-backed to the gaping doorway and off out to pleasanter things, hugging inside yourself the bitter black wild magic of it, and the warm proof of your own courage. Alive, that cat had been nothing; dead, it was a living god of power, our strongest thing. Every time you saw the shape of the mill on the skyline, you went under the power of the cat.

Then there was the day Nana's canary escaped, while she was cleaning its cage. One moment it was doing its usual frantic fluttering from curtain-rail to mantelpiece, and the next minute the wind blew the back door open, and when we looked up, it had gone and the kitchen was coldly quiet and empty. And it was nowhere in sight in the back yard either.

'Botheration,' she said. (I think she would have said something stronger if I hadn't been there.) 'Silly thing. Now it will die of cold or starve. Or the other birds will peck it to death.'

'Why?' I asked, appalled.

''Cos it's different from them, an' they know it's different.'

'What can we do?' I'd never thought about the canary much before; it was just one of her things, like the chiming clock or the polished horse-brasses round the fireplace; but now I was shocked by the suddenness of its fate.

'Go an' look for it. No point in looking around

2

here.' She surveyed the endless vista of soot-blackened, cat-haunted brick walls, dustbins and washing on lines. 'No point lookin' round here. Even the sparrows can't stick it. It'll make for where there's trees. The old cemetery.'

She picked up the newly cleaned cage and made for the door.

'Why you taking that?' I asked.

''Cos by the time we find it, it'll be cold an' hungry an' having second thoughts. It'll take one look at its home an' fly straight in. It'll know where it's well off.'

I followed her obediently. If it had been my mother, walking along the street carrying a birdcage, whistling like a canary every ten yards and calling 'Peter, Peter', I might have had fears that one of my friends might see her and think her crackers.

But Nana was a law unto herself; I'd have followed her *anywhere.*

The old cemetery was nice; not like the new one, with its ghastly endless vista of white tombstones grinning like teeth. The tombstones in the old cemetery were of warm worn sandstone, across which the setting sun slanted, casting the shadows of leaves and branches. The trees were high and densely packed. It seemed a good place for a canary on the run to choose. Nana walked into the spatter of sunlight and green shadow, calling and whistling. I lingered. The carved writing on the tombs was ancient and curious, and took a lot of spelling out, especially where the sun and rain had eaten it away. But I found a master mariner's gravestone, with a carving of his ship in full sail at the top. And a Tyne pilot, and a ship's husband. One tombstone led me to another, along the green glades. I felt quite unafraid, because the place was small, and the wall low, and the sound of passing traffic came to me, and the quick clop of ponies' hooves. Besides the sound of Nana whistling and calling 'Peter'. If I was thinking of anything, I was wondering what a ship's husband could be. How could a man be married to a ship? Was it another word for a captain?

So I got quite a start when I peered round a tall tomb and saw a man sitting, perched on the little wall that ran round a grave.

He was not a tramp, or even a rough sort of man. He wore a suit with a waistcoat and watch-and-chain, and his boots were highly polished and shone like black diamonds. He wore a cap, and was very small and very old. His hair shone, under his cap, like white silver.

And he was talking to a tombstone. He was holding up a new shirt, as if he was showing it to the tombstone. The shirt was soft white flannel, with a thin blue stripe every inch or so.

'Our Doris got it for me in a sale,' he said. 'A fourteen collar, so it should fit all right. Aah hope you like it.' He sounded a bit worried, as if he wanted it approved of. After a bit, he sighed, and put it down on his knees again. Then he said, 'Our Tommy's doing well. They think a lot of him, down at the yard. They've just made him a foreman. . . .' Then, after a bit, he said, 'Young Ada's had the chicken-pox, but she's getting over it nicely.'

4

I wasn't scared. I was just . . . sort of hypnotised. It was all so different. I must confess I jumped when I felt a hand on my shoulder. But not much, because I somehow knew it was Nana's hand. The old man glanced up then; he must have noticed Nana, though he hadn't noticed me.

'Hello, Billy,' said Nana. 'What fettle the day?'

'Not so bad, hinny. Cannit grumble.'

'This is my grandson.'

The little old man reached over and shook hands with me. His hand was soft and dry and warm, but thin like a bird's claw.

'Pleased to meet you.' Then he went on talking to Nana about quite ordinary things, like the lost canary. He said he hadn't seen any canaries flying round this morning, but he'd keep his eye open. Then we said goodbye and walked off, and I heard him say to the tombstone, 'Well that's all for now, pet. I'll see you next week, same as usual. Sorry I was late today, but our Doris kept me, about the shirt.'

'Who's he talking to?' I hissed at Nana.

'His missus,' said Nana comfortably. 'Hetty Stokes as was. Hetty Newman after she married, God rest her. He's a good man – not like some. He never married again, an' it's forty years now. Brought up three bairns on his own, with only his mother to help him . . . . He comes to see her every week. Used to come every day, after she first died.'

'But he *talks* to her!'

'Aye, he still tells her all his troubles.'

'Does she answer him?'

'Aah never asked him. That's between man and

5

wife . . . .' Then she added, 'No bloody sign of that canary. I wonder if it's gone to Dr Seymour's garden . . . .'

She made it all seem so *normal*. A man talking to his wife who'd been dead for forty years; and a lost canary. They were all the same to her. She *accepted* things. I remember her once saying comfortably, 'You'll swallow a peck of dirt before you die,' and I haven't worried about dirt from that day to this. It's those people who wash their hands ten times a day and buy all this stuff for squirting in lavatory pans who seem mad to me.

But I left that churchyard, at the age of nine, with my picture of the dead complete. They were still around, and interested in the everyday doings of the living. They were still part of the family. They lived, in the ground, in their underground town, and gossiped to each other about shirts. And on the Day of Judgement, as our vicar said, they would all emerge, dusting a little soil off their best clothes, and say hello, and shake hands with everybody they knew. It seemed a cosy happy thing to me, just like my own family. Like Great-aunt Dora and Uncle Harry, who were in the old cemetery as well, but whose doings were still told and laughed about at family gatherings like Christmas.

It was five years before I met Valerie; who changed my ideas about death.

Chapter Two

In the first three years at grammar school, they kept the boys and girls apart. Of course, we looked at them, in the corridor, as crocodiles of boys filed past crocodiles of girls. But they all looked the same in their shapeless gym-dresses, like sheep. All but the girl prefects, who wore striped blazers, and blouses that bulged in a fascinating way that made you feel pleasantly sad, and who had shapely brown calves and fashionable hair-styles. They had the power to punish us boys, if they saw us misbehaving, and there was quite a fashion in getting yourself punished by them, and having to take your lines to the girl prefects' room, and knock and ask for *your* prefect. You always tried to get punished by the prefect you had a particular crush on at the time. I chose Hermione Allthorpe, who was the school tennis champion, and who was going up to Cambridge, and who had a long tanned glowing face and large dark eyes. I have seldom since had such a romantic thrill as when being told off by Hermione Allthorpe, and having her slim hand scribble 'Approved H. Allthorpe' in my punishment book. It was like getting a film star's autograph. I expect she just thought of me as a scruffy little tick, though she once said, 'I don't know why you only misbehave when I'm around. The boys' prefects say you're as good as gold.'

I said, 'No fear – the boys' prefects beat you with cricket-stumps.'

And she blushed and closed the prefects' room door quickly.

Anyway, in the fourth year, we actually had boys and girls in the same glass. Four Express they called us, because we were the pick of the bunch, meant to do School Cert in four years instead of five.

We boys sat in a block next to the windows, and stared surreptitiously at the girls as they sat in a block next to the door. Where the two blocks met, our frontier was the dirty boys who told dirty jokes, whom we rather despised. And their frontier was girls whom there were rumours about, who were said to let you do things, whom we despised even more.

Anyway, we stared surreptitiously, but there wasn't a lot to stare at. Any bulges they might be developing were more than lost inside those voluminous gym-slips and their bare legs above white ankle-socks were pale, shapeless, goose-pimpled, blue, scarred or spotty and no more interesting than our own beneath our short trousers. We pronounced them dim beings who were far too keen to put up their hands and answer the teachers' questions, who got uncomfortably high marks for their homework, and who, above all, had neat handwriting which the teachers held up as shining examples. Sickening.

All but one who sat in the front, as far from us boys as possible. She was as shapelessly wrapped as the rest. But she had a beautifully straight nose. And a high intelligent forehead. And enormous luxurious pigtails of red-gold hair, that lay against her pale cheek, and reached right down to where her bulges might have been, if any had been visible. All the vitality that was lacking in her pale, pale cheeks seemed to have gone into that hair. And she loved it so. In lessons, listening to the teacher intently (like all the other girls), she would stroke it with a long pale hand, as if it were a cat on her shoulder. She would rub her cheek against it, for comfort or in sheer pleasure. At times, she would even hold one of the ends against her face, and gently take it into her pale, pale ladylike mouth.

I was fascinated; too fascinated. Ron Berry, sneaky bastard, noticed me looking.

'What you watching that chinless wonder for? Are you in *love* with her?'

My heart stopped. If he got away with that, *years* of agony lay ahead of me. Years of ragging.

'And what, bright-eyes,' I said, 'lies directly in front of her?'

He looked. 'The door?'

'Correct, stupid. And who is lurking on the far side of that glass door? Who occasionally comes through that door and hauls out some kid, and gives him six of the best?'

'Holy Joe,' he said.

'Precisely,' I said. 'And he's walked past twice in the last five minutes, and I think he's making up his mind to come in. He isn't after you, is he? Haven't got a bad conscience, have you?'

He went a trifle pale. Berry always had something

on his conscience, and got caned quite a lot for a top-stream kid. He worried for the rest of the lesson. That'd teach him. Anyway, it got me off the hook. But it taught me to ration my stares at her. Even after the incredible moment when she actually plucked up courage to look across to the boys' side of the room, and I saw what enormous and beautiful grey-green eyes she had. I'd never *seen* such eyes. I thought she looked like the angel in the stained-glass window in our church. A disembodied being a million miles removed from the dirty girls who let you do things to them . . . it was right that she was wrapped in a voluminous gym-slip. It would be sacrilege to expect bulges on her, as it would to expect them on the angel in our church window.

Of course, I finally had to acknowledge that Berry had been right. She was a little lacking in chin; just a bit. But who wants an angel to have a chin like Desperate Dan? It made me feel protective towards her, that slight lack of chin. It was the defect that made the divine human, touchable. Well, not touchable, but *here*. Breathing the same classroom air as me. The thought occurred that several molecules of classroom air that had started the lesson inside her lungs must now be inside *mine*.

The thought made me too slow in answering Moggy Morris's question about strip-farming in the medieval manor, and I got fifty lines for daydreaming.

Mind you, I wasn't exposed to temptation all that often. She was absent more than she was present.

That was how I got to know her name; for it would have been suicide to ask anybody.

'Valerie Monkton?' our form-teacher would call out, reading from the register.

Silence.

Now usually the form-teacher would make a fuss if somebody was absent. Anyone know what's wrong with Mary Jones? Who last saw her? But when it was Valerie, he'd just set his lips and call out the next name. Somehow you could tell they *expected* Valerie to be absent. And somehow, it made my daydreaming about her easier. She wasn't *there* enough to be a real person; so she became somebody whom I could take out of my pocket when I wanted to, and daydream adventures with. Like soldiers carried a photograph of their girlfriend in their wallets. I won't bore you with the daydreams. They usually involved rescuing her from some terrifying peril. Once I'd rescued her, and she'd thanked me gravely, I didn't know quite what to do with her next, so we usually just wandered off into the sunset, like in the movies. In my daydreams she always let me hold her hand. It was long and slim and cool, and could always raise gooseflesh on the back of my neck.

It was therefore a terrible shock when I wandered into the form-room one morning, worrying about the answers to my maths homework, and she was standing by her desk next to the door, and she not only smiled but actually *spoke* to me.

'You're Bob Bickerstaffe, aren't you?' she said. The way she said it, and the way she smiled, I knew she knew something about me that I didn't know.

11

I blushed to the roots of my hair; it felt like a great hot frightening flood of blood; my head spun. I mean, every eye in the class was watching us. The girls *never* spoke to the boys; except the girls who let you do things to them spoke to the boys who told dirty stories about them. . . .

'Yep,' I said, and fled to my desk, face still burning.

'What she say to you?' said the ever sharp-eyed Berry. I think he had eyes in the back of his head.

'She told me my shoe-lace was undone.' I could tell it was undone, because my shoe was feeling loose. Which was just as well, for he looked to make sure.

'And what did you say to her?'

'Told her to mind her own bloody business.'

'She's a bossy little cow. They're all bossy little cows.'

'Yep,' I said, and that was the end of it. Though the memory of it brought me out in a cold sweat for days after.

I had to be extra-careful peeping at her across the room after that. Because she always seemed to be peeping at me, and if our eyes met, she smiled as if she knew me already. And with that hundred-eyed Argus Berry ever-watching, and the other girls, I nearly gave up watching her altogether.

But the daydreams got disturbingly livelier.

One teatime, my Dad looked across the table at me and said, 'You're doing well at school, I hear! Always first wi' the answer.'

I looked across at him warily. School was not Dad's business. The gasworks was Dad's business;

12

he was foreman. School was my business. He got a good school-report every term, and that should have been enough for him.

He had a sly grin on his face. He looked at my Mam. She had a sly grin on her face, too. Parents are unbearable when they go on like that.

'I'm not a swot,' I said.

Swots put up their hands to answer every question, even the easy ones where everybody knows the answer. That's why they get despised; wanting to be teacher's pet.

But sometimes, when the teacher asked a really hard question, and nobody else could get it, I would give them the answer, so we could get on with the wretched lesson. That's different; that gets you respected.

My Mum and Dad were still grinning, in that knowing way. I just can't stand that kind of thing, so I said, 'Who told you?'

'A little bird,' said my mother. Big deal. They always say 'a little bird'. They do it hundreds and thousands of times from when you're about three, but they still think it's funny.

So I said, with a great show of not giving two damns, 'Can I have some bread, please?' as if the subject was closed.

That they can't stand. So my Dad said, 'A young lady.' Big, big grins again. And I blushed as well, curse it.

'I don't know any young ladies.'

'This one knows you.'

'Miss Stringer,' I said with disgust. Miss Stringer

taught English, and my Nana knew her mother, and gossip passed round. Miss Stringer was quite pretty for a teacher, and good fun, but she would open her mouth out of school.

'Not Miss Stringer,' said my Dad. He was really loving this.

'Can I have a piece of bread *please*?'

'Valerie Monkton,' said my Dad.

I nearly went mad. 'You don't *know* Valerie Monkton.'

'I know her father. George Monkton. Our manager.'

'His name's George Munton,' I shrieked in agony.

'No it's not, it's Monkton,' he said smugly. 'I should know. I've worked for him for ten years. And their Valerie knows you at school.' God, parents don't half make a meal of it.

'Can I have a piece of bread, or can't we afford it?'

That got my Mum going with the bread-knife. I munched the bread, while the world whirled round my head.

'Don't fill your mouth so full,' said my mother.

She could get lost! While your mouth's full, you can't be asked to say anything.

This was disastrous. George Monkton and my Dad were big mates. Normally, my Dad can't stand bosses of any description. He calls them bloodsuckers who grow fat on the sweat of the working man. But my Dad said that George Monkton was a good engineer who had come up the hard way by his own efforts. He had a big house at the gasworks gate, and if he was digging his cabbages when my Dad passed on his

14

bike, coming home in the evening, Dad would stop and they would have a crack.

'Valerie thinks you're a very nice boy,' said my mother. 'She says you have very nice manners. I wish we saw some of them round here.'

This was *insufferable*. I'd been thinking all the time that Valerie Monkton had been in my pocket, and now I was suddenly in hers. And she was doing it in public. It was worse than that dream you have, when you're walking down the street saying hello to your mates and your mates' parents, and suddenly you realise you're not wearing any trousers.

'Do you like Valerie?' asked my mother.

'We never think about the girls,' I said firmly. 'Girls are useless, stupid, and no good at games. Our rugby team played the girls' hockey team at hockey, and they won three-nil. And they'd never played hockey before in their *lives*.'

'Aye,' said my Dad. He had a way of drawing his breath in when he said 'aye', which was always bad news. 'Poor Valerie won't be playing any hockey.'

Suddenly all their teasing was gone, and it was as if the room had gone cold.

'What's the matter with her?' I asked.

'Never you mind,' said my mother. 'Get on with your tea. How much homework have you got tonight?'

Chapter Three

It was about that time that Miss Stringer tried to teach us a poem by Alfred, Lord Tennyson called 'The Lady of Shalott'.

That was a bad mistake. For one thing, shallots, for us, were small onions that our fathers grew in their back gardens. Berry was quick with the sharp cracks about the Lady of Onions and did she cry a lot when she was peeling them, and did she belong to a Trade Onion? Deedah, deedah, deedah. Very boring.

But worse, the poem was so soppy, the girls loved it and the lads really hated it. It was about this female who sits all day weaving a tapestry and watching the world pass, through a mirror, because if she looked the world straight in the face she'd die. I mean, it hadn't got a lot to do with beating Hitler, had it? We lads asked Miss Stringer a lot of awkward questions like how did she cook and eat, and how did she go to the loo? You can hardly do that in a mirror . . .

Then we got to the bit where the bold Sir Lancelot came riding by on his horse, on his way down to Camelot. Berry said was he called Sir Lancelot because he used his lance a lot? And we had a lad in the class whose second name was Lancelot and we knew it, so it was hard luck on him too. Berry asked him where he tethered his sturdy charger, and could he have the horse-manure for his dad's allotment? And when the unfortunate Lancelot tried to answer back, Berry told him to shut his visor . . .

Miss Stringer had to spend some time restoring order, before she could go on reading.

Anyway, apparently this lady was so entranced by Sir Lancelot that she left her mirror and *looked down to Camelot*. Miss Stringer paused at this point, for dramatic effect. Which was also a mistake.

'Stupid Cow,' said Berry. Sotto voce, but not sotto voce enough. I'm sure he meant the Lady of Shalott and not Miss Stringer, because he added, 'She'll have her Trade Onion after her for that.' But it was too late. Miss Stringer slung him out of the room into the corridor, and Holy Joe picked him up within five minutes and gave him three of the best, we later learnt.

Miss Stringer, relieved of Berry's presence, pressed on with the poem.

' "The curse is come upon me,' cried The Lady of Shalott." '

All the girls began giggling and sniggering, in a secret blushing sort of way. Then Miss Stringer blushed herself, and told the girls angrily not to be stupid, and all us boys were totally baffled about what was going on, even the dirty-minded ones, though they reckoned later it was *something* about sex.

Miss Stringer struggled on to the point where the Lady had scrambled into her handily moored boat, and drifted down the river singing, and died, and come to the city of Camelot, and is being looked at by the aforesaid Sir Lancelot. I mean, it was about as realistic as an advert for Pears' soap. And yet it made us lads feel *uneasy*. On she went:

' "But Lancelot mused a little space; He said . . ." '

Miss Stringer took off her spectacles, which she sometimes did, and stared at us expectantly. She looked really pretty without her spectacles, in a flushed defenceless sort of way, that made me glad Berry wasn't around.

'Now what do you think Sir Lancelot said about the Lady?'

Long silence. Then Billy Brownlee said, ' "That's Shalott!" I mean, "That's yer lot!" See? It's a joke, miss.'

He said the latter defensively as Miss Stringer, still not wearing her spectacles, sallied forth down his aisle and hit him over the head with the collected works of Alfred, Lord Tennyson. And Alfred must have written a lot of stuff; it was a very thick book, and not Miss Stringer's normal sort of behaviour at all.

Then she went back to her seat and said, with tears in her eyes and looking more defenceless than ever, 'I am trying to show you boys something *beautiful* and all you can do is make stupid jokes about it.'

There was total awful silence then, because she really was very upset, and we really did like her, and everyone felt odd and uncomfortable, because some rule had been broken that wasn't in the Rules of the School.

After a while, she went on more quietly, and we tried to be good and helpful

'What do you think of it all, Bickerstaffe?' She

knew she could rely on me to be reasonable and not make stupid jokes. Maybe because her mother knew my grandmother. Maybe because she knew that, deep down, I wasn't really cruel like some people I could name. . . .

I wanted to help her; but that didn't mean I was giving up common sense.

'It's not realistic,' I said. 'Tennyson doesn't tell us who put the curse on her, or why, or how she could get out of it. And she knew the rules. Why did she break them? She *knew* what would happen.'

Miss Stringer looked at me, and sighed. 'Oh, what an old head you have on young shoulders, Bickerstaffe. So *sensible*. The Lady broke the rules because she saw someone . . . she wanted to know better. She knew the rules, but she no longer cared what happened to her. She wanted *life* to happen to her. So the rules weren't important any more. You'll learn, Bickerstaffe. It will happen to *you*, one day.'

That really wasn't fair of her. All the girls turned and looked at me; and all the boys fell about in their desks, laughing.

But it was Miss Stringer's face I kept looking at. It was her, and yet it wasn't her. Her face was all lit up, as if she had a light inside her, and it made me feel all churned up inside, no matter how much I tried to force the feeling down.

Thank God the bell went then. Miss Stringer put on her spectacles and swept out of the room without setting any homework. And Billy Brownlee called across, 'You'll *learn*, Bickerstaffe! It'll happen to *you* one day,' in such a sneery voice that I threw

19

my copy of *The White Company* by Sir Arthur Conan Doyle at him, and it split in two when it hit him in the face, and then we had a right punch-up, all the boys. A really wild punch-up, much worse than usual. And Denny Twiggs, the deputy head boy, who was passing had a hell of a job breaking it up, and gave us all two hundred lines each.

All my life, that lesson has stuck in my mind.

First because I asked Nana what had made Miss Stringer go all lit up and crazy like that, and she said she'd just got engaged to a fighter pilot. I couldn't believe that love could do that to a woman.

Or death either. Because Miss Stringer's bloke was killed in a crash three months later, long before the war started. And she came back for the new term with all her lovely hair cut off, and she wore her spectacles all the time and you could hardly recognise her as the same person. Her light had gone out for ever.

The other reason I remember 'The Lady of Shalott' is Valerie Monkton.

Things moved pretty quickly after that, because Mrs Monkton 'made herself known' to my mother, at our Townswomen's Guild. Mrs Monkton was pronounced a nice lady. 'Very affable.' And Mrs Monkton was worried about Valerie. Having to spend so much time alone at home. Because she was 'delicate'. I should have seen it coming, but I didn't, because it was so much against all the rules I lived by. I don't think my father would ever have done it to me, but mothers are different; mothers are sneaky, and they are never so sneaky as when they think they are doing good.

I sat down to tea one night, all unsuspecting. (Everything important in our house seemed to happen over tea.) My mother gave my father a look, and he gave her one back, and I knew something was coming. I couldn't tell whether it was good or bad, but it was plotty. Then my mother said, very matter-of-fact, 'Valerie has invited you to go to tea.'

I can tell you, the ground just opened up beneath me. I mean, it broke all the rules. The Monktons were posh; they had a car. And a telephone. In spite of Dad's chats over the cabbages and Mum at the Townswomen's Guild, they just weren't our *sort*. They would use serviettes, which always fell off my lap in cafés, making me grovel on the floor just when the waitress came. They would have vast arrays of knives and forks, and I was bound to use the wrong one.

But that was just the start. If the lads at school got a word of it . . .

I told them no. Never. Not in a million years. Then I dashed off to my bedroom, leaving half my bacon and eggs uneaten. That should have impressed them with the degree of my agony, if anything did.

I lay on my bedspread and *writhed*. But I knew all along I'd have to go. I had no choice. Anything less would be a deadly insult to the Monktons. My Dad might even get the sack . . .

I thought I would go, once, and play it dead wooden. Nothing that anyone could object to. I would just be so boring that Valerie wouldn't dream of asking me again. Then I went out and said I would go, and my Mum got my bacon and eggs back out of the oven, almost dry and baked to the plate with waiting, and I levered them off the plate and ate them, thinking 'the condemned man ate a hearty meal'.

There were only two panics after that. The first was what I should say, if any of the lads saw me going into the Monktons' house. That proved fairly easy; I would say I was taking Mr Monkton a note about the works from my Dad.

The second panic was about what I was going to wear. My mother wanted to take me out to buy a posh suit, with long trousers, which was ridiculous, because I was shooting up like a beanstalk at that time. I was always being told I was very hard to keep in clothes, even school uniform.

In the end, I went in my school uniform, pressed to within an inch of its life, and with my black shoes as polished as the old man's boots that day long ago in the cemetery. And in my pocket, done up with a bow, a little present for Valerie that my mother had bought, that must have been scent, because the wrapping ponged so much.

Nobody saw me on the walk; though from the way I glared around and felt tempted to hide behind trees, I wonder I wasn't arrested as a spy.

After I rang the Monktons' doorbell, I had that terrible temptation to run away, like you get after you've rung the dentist's bell.

Mrs Monkton opened the door. She was tall and slim; much younger-looking and more glamorous than my mother. She shook hands and said she was *very* pleased to meet me at last, she'd heard so much about me from Valerie. I couldn't think of anything to say at all, which is not like me; so I merely put a look on my face like a simpering sheep that has suddenly discovered it wants to go to the toilet. Then Mr Monkton appeared and shook me warmly by the hand. And said he was pleased to meet me at last, he'd heard so much about me from Valerie. He was a large bear-like man with a beard like the late King George the Fifth. He looked sort of noble, and wore a very hairy brown suit with a waistcoat. He had very large hands; mine just sort of vanished inside his.

Then no one could think of anything to say. I wondered if I should ask him how his cabbages were; but it was early spring, not really the time for cabbages. I wondered if I should ask him how the gasworks was, but that seemed too personal. Then Mrs Monkton started to ask me how I was getting on at school, only, halfway through, Mr Monkton also started to ask me how I was getting on at school, and they sort of collided and stopped. So I started to tell them how boring maths was and went on and on, though I was quite sure no one was listening. Not even me.

Because I was getting totally fascinated by the entrance-hall we were standing in. It was as big and dark as a church, with the white staircase winding up round three sides. The floor was black and white squares, and there was a big pointed window on the staircase landing. By the light coming from it, I could see a statue in white marble, as big as a real woman, and absolutely stark naked, except for something like a towel which didn't hide much. I couldn't take my eyes off it, till I sensed Mrs Monkton was watching me, when I transferred my gaze hurriedly to a very large aspidistra in a brass pot.

'That's a very big aspidistra,' I said.

Whereupon they both burst out laughing. So infectiously that I had to start laughing too. I mean, we just laughed and laughed, and we all knew what we were really laughing about, though nobody said anything. Then I managed to say, 'My grandmother's got an aspidistra nearly as big,' when we all went off laughing again. That aspidistra joke lasted as long as I knew the Monktons; it never wore out; it got us out of many an awkward corner.

We were still laughing off and on when Valerie's voice said, 'What's everybody laughing about?' She sounded a bit cross, because we'd started laughing without waiting for her. She came down the stairs, against the light, a tall thin figure.

'Bob's been admiring our aspidistra,' said her father. Then he said, a bit more strictly, 'You should have been here to welcome your guest.'

'Oh, she's spent hours titivating her face,' said her mother. '*Vain* little thing. You girls are all the same. You think of nothing else.'

I thought then her voice was like a three-decker sandwich; the sort we only saw in Popeye cartoons in American comics. On top, it was a sort of scolding, but underneath that there was a gladness that Valerie was acting like other girls. And under that . . . a fear, that nearly made my own heart stop beating. That was the first time I heard the pretend in the Monktons' voices. It was new to me, and it scared me. In our family, we didn't pretend, ever. If we were angry, we shouted at each other; once my Dad even threw the Sunday roast beef on the fire in a rage. (Though my Mum quickly got it off again, even at the expense of burning her fingers, and we ate it, or most of it, when we had all got the rage out of our systems.) If we were sad, like when the dog had to be put down, we wept, even my Dad. And when we were happy, we sang (though my Dad could never sing in tune, which caused a lot of laughs). But the Monktons pretended all the time. I suppose they had to, to go on living.

Anyway, now Valerie pirouetted gently around. 'Do I look nice?'

And you had to admit she did. Her marvellous red-gold hair hung straight down her back, brushed clear of her high pale forehead. Her brand-new Angora cardigan, with its big collar turned up round her long pale neck, was soft and fluffy, and the exact colour of her grey-green eyes. The sleeves were pushed up to her elbows, and on one thin wrist was a gold wrist-watch, and on the other, a thick gold bracelet. She was wearing pink nail-varnish, very ladylike, and her nails were longer than most girls had them. And she was wearing stockings I swear were real silk, and high-heeled shoes, like a grown-up woman.

'A real fairy-tale princess,' said her father, and she gave him a lovely warm smile.

'You've been at my nail-varnish,' said her mother; but her voice lacked all bite.

'And what have you got to say for yourself, Bob Bickerstaffe?' she said to me. 'You're very quiet! For you!'

'You look smashing,' I said.

'*Men!*' she said. 'I spend two hours making myself look pretty for you, and all you can say is "smashing". Like I was a Dinky Toy you'd been saving up your pocket-money for.'

That got another laugh. And then her father said, 'Why don't you show Bob the garden, while we get the tea?'

'Will you be warm enough?' her mother asked her anxiously.

'Oh, Mother, don't fuss.'

The garden staggered me. I mean, my Dad was always a keen gardener; he liked his privet hedge and a well-mown lawn in front, and his rows of cabbages and turnips behind. But this garden was totally different.

It had a magnificent view. The gasworks sat on its steep hill above the river, like some great red-brick cathedral, with a ten-foot wall around it. The manager's house was just outside the main gate, and the garden ran along the river side, with the gasworks wall sheltering it from the north-east gales. It fell in a series of steps and terraces towards the river, ending at the bottom with another high wall. Beyond the wall was the scene I knew and loved: the great harbour between its long piers, and below us the Fish Quay with its trawlers, and the welders at Smith's Dock sending streams of brilliant blue sparks falling like fireworks.

But the garden seemed so private; as if we could see the trawlermen and the welders working, but they couldn't see us staring down at them.

And the things in the garden: white marble urns with little trees in them, two more statues of near-starkers ladies, and a summer-house made of tree-branches with the bark still on them, that you could turn on its base to catch the best of the sun, Valerie said. Everything was a bit sooty; Valerie always wiped the benches with a cloth before she would sit down anywhere, but it was beautifully kept.

We wandered around, me saying things like 'That's London Pride, my Dad's got some of that,' and she telling me the Latin names for all the plants I'd never seen before. And neither of us looking the other in the face, as if we were opposing armies crouching in our trenches, each one frightened to emerge and go into the attack. In the end, when she had run out of Latin names, we went and sat in the summer-house, side by side. I could see her hands were trembling; I wondered if she felt the cold, though it was not at all a cold day, really. Quite springlike, in fact. Then there was another terrible long silence, because neither of us could think of anything to say any more.

Finally, she said, in a low desperate voice, 'You didn't mind me inviting you?'

I looked at her then; and she looked at me. Her lips were trembling as well. I felt so many things. Here was my angel, close enough to touch. Her eyes were just as huge and beautiful as when she had first looked across the classroom at me; her nose was still as straight. But now I had her, I was no longer sure I wanted her. What I wanted was to daydream about her, to admire her from a distance. Close to, she was too *real*. And she looked so *helpless*. Half of me wanted to protect her, and half of me wanted to hurt her, to say something to make her cry. Because I was very angry at her cheek in summoning me; at her using her father to get at my father; at the danger she was putting me in with Ron Berry and that lot.

It was the anger that won. I said, 'If Ron Berry finds out about this, my life won't be worth living.'

'What does it matter, what he thinks?'

'You've seen what they're like; how they rag people. Fat lads, thin lads. They rag me because my ears stick out. If they find out about this, they'll *crucify* me.'

She bit her pale pink lip. 'I'm sorry. *I* won't tell anybody.'

'Not even your girlfriends?'

'Promise. I hardly ever see them.'

'And what about your mother? At the Townswomen's Guild. You *know* how they gossip . . .'

'I'll ask Mummy not to mention a word.'

She was so humble; so desperate. It made me want to go on being fierce with her. 'And what about your father?'

Her eyes suddenly turned very bright. Her bottom eyelids filled up with . . . God, she was going to cry. If she cried, I'd get the blame. From the Monktons. From my Mum and Dad . . . *Anything* to stop her. I remembered what my Dad said to my Mum. I said, 'I'll scratch your back, if you'll scratch mine.'

'Oh, yes please,' she said, and burst out laughing. When I looked again for the tears, they were nowhere to be seen. Oh, the mysteries of woman.

I looked back at the river, all shaky at the knees

at disaster averted. Saw a familiar ship, with two black funnels with white stripes, heading briskly down the river, under the bossy whooping charge of two tugboats.

'That's the *Venus*,' I said. 'The mail ship, going to Norway.'

'I know *that*,' she said, a bit annoyed. Then looked at me anxiously, terrified she'd dropped a clanger.

I don't like anybody cowering to me like that. So I said, 'If the mail ships go to Norway, where do the female ships go to?' It was an old joke. I don't know if she'd heard it before. But she was careful to laugh.

Just then, her father came down the steps, calling out that tea was ready. He looked anxious, till he saw us sitting side by side, then he looked relieved and grinned and said, 'What were you two laughing about?' When she told him, he said, 'That old joke! We had that joke when I was a lad. I'm glad it's still going . . .'

And we went in to tea.

It was a really smashing tea, with sandwiches made with the new sliced bread, and shop cakes covered with yellow and pink and green icing. And a jelly in the shape of a rabbit with its ears laid back. It was quite easy, with no silences, because her father did nearly all the talking. And the serviettes weren't those awful paper ones that fall off your knee, but big thick white linen ones that lie on your legs quite snug. And there was only one little knife each, with a purple handle, to cut your cakes and sandwiches with, and a spoon for the jelly, so I soon had that worked out.

Her father was a very interesting man, who'd knocked round the world a bit as a ship's engineer, before he settled down. He'd been up the Persian Gulf, and been to one of those Arab feasts where the sheikhs suddenly offer you a sheep's eye, and you have to eat it, without throwing up. I could see why my father liked talking to him.

I kept my end up, asking if the sheep's eye was cooked or raw, and whether you put salt on it, before you ate it, till her Mum cried, 'Oh, *don't*. You men are *awful*. You're all alike,' and Valerie punched me on the arm, though very gently. We all laughed a lot. Till somebody mentioned Hitler.

I don't think anybody meant to. It was just that all that spring and summer of 1939, he kept creeping into everything, like the smell from the town's guano-works.

'What do you think of Hitler, then, Bob?' said her father, suddenly serious, and man-to-man. I thought hard; I wanted to sound grown-up.

'He'll not stop,' I said at last, 'till somebody gives him a bloody nose. He's like the class bully. Always picking on the little kids, till one of the big kids thumps him.'

'Out of the mouths of babes and sucklings,' said her father, almost to himself. His eyes weren't looking at anything; he played with his knife, drawing lines with it in the thick white tablecloth.

I didn't want to sound like a babe, and I didn't like the sound of sucklings, though I wasn't quite sure what they were. So I said, 'We could do it. We beat them last time. The British Empire is a hundred times the size of them. The British Navy will blockade them, and they'll run out of rubber an' copper an' tin and oil. They've got nothing *now*. They have to roast acorns because they can't afford real coffee. Their soldiers have boots with paper soles. Hitler's a nutter . . . when he gets mad he foams at the mouth and chews the carpet.'

He gave me a look that silenced me with its sadness. 'And what about you?'

'I'd join the RAF and fly Spitfires,' I said. 'If the war lasts that long.' It's easy to be brave, when you're fourteen.

Valerie gave a tiny female scream, which was not displeasing. Her mother turned quite pale, which was not displeasing either.

'Well,' said her father, moving suddenly out of his stillness with false heartiness. 'Who's for another cup of tea?'

I left soon afterwards; I had a feeling I'd cast a blight over a happy day.

Chapter Four

The sun always seemed to be shining, that last summer of peace. My father tried to join the RAF, as an aero-engine fitter. My Mam and he had a row about it, after I was in bed. I remember her yelling that he was a married man, with responsibilities and a child. He kept yelling back that his country needed him. Anyway, he went for a medical, and his country found he had varicose veins, and didn't need him after all. Otherwise, I avidly collected the new cigarette cards that were coming out. Wills' Capstan brand, which my Dad smoked, were doing a series on 'Air-raid Precautions' and Player's, which Valerie's dad smoked, were doing 'Aircraft of the RAF', so I did pretty well out of it. I think I wanted there to be a war, otherwise all the cigarette cards, and all the new Spitfires that were pouring off the production lines, would be wasted.

At school, everyone was practising doing the Nazi goose-step, and getting pushed over by their mates for their pains. And combing their hair down in a forelock, and sticking a rubber under their nose, and holding their right arm in the air, and doing impersonations of Hitler.

Otherwise, I kept up my secret life with Valerie. I had her well trained by now. She was at school a lot, because it was the summer term, but she never looked across the classroom at me any more. And she'd certainly closed her mother's mouth (I had no real worry about her father) because there wasn't a whisper about us anywhere. I would sit in the classroom and throw a secret glance at her, and then glance at the loathsome Berry, and think, 'If only you knew, mate, if only you *knew*,' and feel smug.

Of course, her mother talked to my mother. About what a nice boy I was, with nice manners. And about how good I was for Valerie, and how she was much better, and putting on a little weight. And my parents were pleased with me for a change, and my Mum nagged me less about muddy shoes and tearing the backside out of my second-best trousers.

I went down to Valerie's a lot, Saturday afternoons and some sunny weekday evenings. I liked the big house, and all the strange things that Mr Monkton had brought back from his travels; the Arab daggers and the Burmese wooden elephants and the Turkish hubble-bubble pipes, or hookahs, as he called them. He always had some yarn to spin about them.

And her parents were always so pleased to see me. More than any of the parents of the girlfriends I had later. And I felt I was doing a bit of good in the world. It was all so *snug* in that garden. We never went anywhere else. She wasn't encouraged to go out for walks, and she never came to our house. Which suited me fine, considering the nosy old bags who lived in our street, going yak-yak-yak all the time, and the fact that Alan Whitaker, Berry's best mate, lived at number nine. My secret would have been out in five minutes.

What did we do in the garden? We talked. Mainly, I talked. She was a good listener, though if I talked too long about Spitfires and Heinkels and Messerschmitts she would go very silent. So then, to cheer her up, I'd talk about the view from the garden; the harbour. She knew it as a view, but I knew it like the back of my hand. The ship-repair yards, where the riveters sounded like a hundred machine-guns, and the apprentices spent their lunchtime throwing spoilt rivets at tin cans floating in the river. The Fish Quay, where the men from the trawlers shouted at you in wild Scottish accents and boys with no shoes fished for blackjack with bent pins, and fish lay crushed under the wheels of the horse-drawn fishcarts. Or the ice factory, where blocks of ice a yard long, gleaming transparent grey, came sliding down the ice-chute. Or the Fish Quay Sands, where the rotting fish-heads snarled at you with long yellow teeth, and the gulls, big as geese, fought with the local tom-cats for the spoils of the fish-gutting. Or the north pier, which you could walk along, dodging the waves as they broke over it. She would end up quite breathless with excitement, her cheeks flushed a most becoming pink.

'I wish I could see it all,' she would say. 'I _do_ wish I could.'

Until the day came when her parents left us alone in the garden, to go shopping, and I looked at the little door at the far end of the garden, and said, 'Why not?'

She looked at me, with her grey-green eyes flaring wide, and her lips a little parted, showing the tips of her top teeth in a very touching way. She went pale, and put her long slim hand to her chest. 'Daddy says . . . the doctor thinks . . .'

'We needn't go far,' I said, coaxingly.

Then she said, 'Why not?' and her cheeks glowed.

The gate at the far end of the garden had a handle so stiff it nearly finished our adventure there and then. But I got it open at last, with a great deal of grunting and sweating, and we were out on the open bankside.

I *did* take care of her; the moment we got outside the garden, care fell on me like a heavy blanket. While she was in the garden, she was her parents' responsibility; once outside, she was mine. I hadn't a clue what her mysterious illness was, or what the warning signs were. And somehow, it was not the time to ask her. She was lit up with freedom and mischief; her huge grey eyes shone, her cheeks were full of colour; she suddenly made all the other girls I'd seen look like dull puddings.

'How do we get down to the Fish Quay?'

I shook my head. The Fish Quay and the Low Street that led to it was a rough old place. Even the policemen went in pairs. At any moment you could be faced with a drunken sailor who would try to embrace you, mouthing obscenities. Or you might be surrounded by a crowd of jabbering lascars, wanting God knew what. And there were the Maltese café-people, in their loud two-tone shoes and broad-brimmed felt hats, who carried knives and knew how to use them. Many a time I'd got out of trouble by taking to my heels. I wasn't risking her down there.

But I could take her along the Bank Top. A hundred feet above the Low Street, only fifty towards the end, but what a difference a few feet can make. It was an area of respectable yellow-brick terraces where the older, staider people lived. Including Nana. Even three-year-olds could wander in safety alone. But you could see everything that happened in the Low Street, as if you were in the gallery of a theatre.

So we strolled in the sun along the Bank Top. I showed her the dry-dock, where a lightship, red as a pillar-box, was being repainted, held upright only by beams that looked as thin as matchsticks. I showed her Purdie's Warehouse, where kittiwakes nested on every windowsill in a raucous Parliament; the Blue Café that was sin HQ for the whole town. And the trawlers lying three-deep at the quayside, sending up their sooty clouds of funnel-smoke to kipper us. We went on and on, from wonder to wonder, me never stopping talking and her never stopping smiling. We crossed the gully, where the cobbled road plunged down to the quay from the upper town, over a narrow footbridge that always made you feel delightfully dizzy, and she held on to my hand like a little bairn. Her hand was just as long and slim and cool as it had felt in my daydreams; and it did bring me out in goose-pimples. We were drunk on each other and on sunlight and adventure. It was a new world for both of us.

She had got her eye on the High Light, the lighthouse that, lined up with the Low Light on the Fish Quay below, guided ships safely into harbour. It was tall, old and beautiful, shining buff and white in the sun. She would walk as far as the High Light.

But at the High Light, the clouds came across the sun, and she suddenly said she felt a little tired.

I looked at her. Was the sparkle fading from her eyes? There was still colour in her cheeks, but was there so much? Had little marks tightened round her mouth?

We started back. It had seemed nothing, coming. Now, under the darkening cloudy sky, it seemed a very long way. The joys of the outward journey now seemed like milestones, mountain peaks to be climbed. I was glad as each one was passed, and the huge chimneys of the gasworks drew nearer.

On the footbridge, she seemed to sway, and I grabbed her without thinking. That was the first time I ever had my arm round a girl. Even in my sudden fright, it was nice.

'Keep your arm there,' she said. 'It's comfy.'

We made better time. She wasn't heavy, and I was a big strong lad for my age, and it was fascinating, the feel of a girl walking inside my arm. Luckily, I knew that none of the mob from school lived round here. Berry's granny did, but Berry and his crowd would be at the football match, screeching insults at the referee, the opposing side, our home side, and anything else that moved.

She seemed even to grow lighter, as we neared home; her sparkle came back, as we reached the green gate, and we went through it laughing, and closed it with a sigh of relief, and went and sat in the summer-house. Once she was safely sitting down, I took my arm away.

She pouted. 'Don't you *like* putting your arm round me?'

'Your Dad might come.'

'I can hear Daddy coming a mile off. Like a herd of elephants . . .'

She could, too. Her hand swiftly removed my hand and put it firmly in my lap, a full minute before her father appeared to tell us it was time for tea.

'You two look very pleased with each other,' he said. 'What have you been up to?'

'Bob's been telling me all about the dry-dock and the lightship. And the kittiwakes on Purdie's. And Annie Stagg.'

I blushed. Annie Stagg was the town's madam; her brothel was famous. But I could tell she was teasing him. She was still pretty high.

I thought she'd gone too far, for a moment. He frowned a bit. But he couldn't hold the frown, because he was so glad to see her lit up and happy. And as my Nana would've said, she could twist him round her little finger . . .

'Well,' he said, with a wry grin, 'I suppose it's a change from Hitler and Spitfires.'

I suppose she twisted me round her little finger as well. My arm was now at her command; she liked it round her most of the time, when her parents weren't about. Sometimes she would say, 'Put your arm round me, I'm cold,' and shiver. Even in the hottest weather. Sometimes she would just grab it and drape it round her without a word, as if it was a favourite scarf.

One day she said, quite matter-of-fact, as we were sitting alone in the summer-house, 'Would you like to kiss me?' and held her face up, with her eyes shut. I thought about it a bit too long, and then kissed her on the cheek, as I might have kissed my mother or an aunt.

'Pooh,' she said. 'That's not much of a kiss. My father can do better than that.' She still hadn't moved; she still had her eyes shut. 'On the mouth, stupid.'

I shuffled uneasily on the seat. I wondered whether her mysterious illness was infectious. There was a lot of illness among kids in those days. A lot of kids caught diphtheria and scarlet fever, and got sent away to the Isolation Hospital, way out in the country beyond Billing's Mill. We used to go past the Isolation Hospital on our explorings, when I was younger; we always ran past the entrance with our mouths tight shut and trying not to breathe through our nostrils, in case a germ came out and got us.

Still, her father kissed her, and he seemed hale and hearty, so I risked it. Her cheek was very soft and downy, and her lips were a lovely shape, as if someone had carved them carefully, with a very small chisel.

'Mmmmmmmm,' she said appreciatively. And then her tongue darted into my mouth, like a small hot deadly snake. I drew back in a kind of warm panic.

'That's called French kissing,' she said, with a wicked glint in her eye. 'I read about it in one of

39

Mummy's books – the ones she keeps under the biscuit-tin in the sideboard. That I'm not supposed to know about.'

'I don't think we ought to do that sort of thing,' I said, sounding as prim as my own mother.

'Whyever not?'

'We're too young,' I said, shuffling uncomfortably again. It was not that I disliked the feelings I was having exactly. It was that I didn't like her causing effects in me that I wasn't in charge of. I've always liked to be entirely in charge of myself.

'It's all right for you,' she said. 'Saying you're too young. You're going to grow up some day. Unless you do something stupid down your Fish Quay. Like getting drowned. Or else flying your stupid Spitfires . . .' She was staring out down the river, out to sea. A patch of colour burned in her smooth cheek like a tiny angry fire.

'Well . . .?' I said indignantly. 'So are you!'

'Am I?' she said, still not looking at me; her voice low and a bit scary. 'I heard the doctor, talking to Mummy. I was listening when I shouldn't have been. He said I wouldn't make old bones.'

I'd heard that phrase often enough; my Nana was always using it. But only about middle-aged men who drank, and wheezed as they walked. Middle-aged men with grey wrinkled faces who spat on the pavement at street-corners, and had nothing to do with me. Another world.

But to say it about her . . . the straight nose, that tilted up just a delightful trace at the end; the downy cheek, the huge eyes. She looked so terribly sad and

40

alone and brave. I couldn't help myself wriggling my bottom back along the seat, and putting both arms around her, and saying, comforting, 'My Nana says children can grow out of illnesses . . . .'

'Stop talking about things you don't understand and give me another kiss, stupid!'

We stayed there a long time, till we heard her father calling us, from the French window of the house. From that time on, he never walked down the garden to call us, just yelled from the house. And looked at us, anxiously, as we walked in.

But as that last summer spun past in sunlight, and my fifteenth birthday came and went (Valerie gave me a large magnifying glass I still have), his anxieties seemed groundless. Valerie came to school every day and was never even late. And in spite of all the work she'd missed earlier, she came seventh in the summer exams. Her father called us a pair of geniuses, because I'd come top as usual. And when her parents went out shopping in the car on Saturday afternoons, we explored further and further along the Bank Top. Once we even met my Nana, and she asked us home for a cup of tea (only it turned into cocoa, because Valerie said she liked cocoa better). Nana had been doing one of her prodigious bakings, and Valerie, for once, ate like a horse, instead of her usual toying with an iced cake.

'I like a lass as likes her vittles,' said Nana, with great approval. And then told us how Field-Marshal Douglas Haig had been a great one for the ladies, during the last war. I remember Valerie now, sitting in Nana's rocker, with her head on her hand, flushed by the heat of the range and laughter. She shared Nana's liking for scandal. And I sat and watched my two women, one each side of the fireplace, and imagined how Nana must have looked when she was Valerie's age, and how Valerie would look when she was Nana's age . . . .

But better still I remember our last expedition but one; to the Priory ruins on the clifftop at the end of Bank Top; the clifftop where the coastguard station was, and the guns that defended the Tyne from the sea, and where the graves of the clipper captains are, who brought the tea back from China in a hundred days. I was all for showing off the guns, and the great range-finders in their concrete towers. But it was the tombs that took Valerie's fancy. Most of them were so old that the frost and the rain and the north-east gales had worn the lettering into strange unreadable whorls like worm-casts. But sometimes, when the setting sun was at the right angle, you could still see a ghost of the lettering, and even read a few words.

'Master and mariner,' she said, almost to herself, 'of the clipper-ship *Phoebe*. Died 1901 aged 92. He *was* old.'

'It's the bracing sea air,' I said, trying to make a joke of it, shake her out of her strange mood.

'And in memory of his dearly beloved daughter, Maude Eliza, died March 11 1854, aged seventeen years . . . fancy living on all those years without his daughter.'

'He probably had a lot of other kids,' I said, a bit brutally. 'They had dozens in those days.' I hated her going on like that.

42

She turned on me fiercely, cheeks burning. 'And don't you think he missed her just the same, even if he did have other kids? Do you think they bred with no more feelings than rabbits?'

'Sorry,' I said, not knowing what else to say. She went back to trying to decipher the lettering, and I just hung about.

I heard her say, 'I'd like to be buried here. On the clifftop, where I could hear the wind and the waves breaking.' In a dreamy voice, half to herself.

And then I saw Councillor Hilda Burridge JP and her tiny husband walking straight towards us, through the tombstones. There was no mistaking the massive figure, in her long black coat and floral hat even in the height of summer. She was a great character in the town, ran the local porkshop, and knew everybody. She knew even more people than my Nana. . . .

And worst of all, young Burridge was Berry's best mate.

There was no time to say a word. Thank God Councillor Burridge was glaring down at the tall grass between the tombstones, pointing it out to her husband with the tip of her black umbrella, and no doubt getting ready to make a complaint about it at the next meeting of the council. But she might look up at any moment, and she was only ten yards away.

I was close to the corner of the Lady Chapel, and I slipped behind it like a ghost.

Tynemouth Priory was a great place for hide-and-seek; though if the curator saw you at it, he would certainly stop you and throw you out. There weren't just the tombstones to hide behind. The ruins were a cluster of worn, tall, vertical bits of sandstone. Single pillars, stumps of walls full of holes and windows. You could watch for ever, if you were careful, without being seen.

Now, I watched. I watched Councillor Mrs Burridge, as she found fault in turn with the mowing of the grass, the seagull droppings on the tombs, the peeling paint on the gate to the coastguard station, a passing tanker sailing out of the Tyne, and no doubt the clouds in the sky. I watched her husband, well trained to tut-tut to order.

But I had to watch Valerie as well. I saw the look on her face, as she first turned and saw that I was gone. I saw her increasing bafflement, as she called my name. I saw her try to believe I was fooling with her, teasing her by hiding. The attempts at hope, the attempts to tell herself she was being silly. I saw her wilt before my eyes, as her alarm turned to distress. She turned this way and that, biting her lip, not knowing what to do. I could've wept. I tried waving to her through window-gaps, when Councillor Burridge wasn't looking, but in her panic she was no longer really searching for me anywhere. She was just going around in circles like a lost cat.

It seemed forever before Councillor Burridge found her last fault and departed. Though I doubt it was more than five minutes. She wasn't there to enjoy the view; she was preparing a complaint to the Parks and Sands Committee; she moved away saying loudly that she was going to give the Town Clerk hell.

I stepped out in front of Valerie. She was in

such a state she nearly walked straight past me. I had to put out my hands to grab her, and she gave a little scream before she realised who I was. Then she said, 'I thought you'd run away and left me.' And burst into tears.

I sat her down on the sunny side of a tomb, and tried to cheer her up. I was worried, because for the first time she seemed oddly breathless. As if she'd run a mile.

'Never do that to me again,' she said, and she wasn't fooling. 'I was terrified. Listen to my heart beating.'

She pulled my head down to her jumper. I could hear her heart fluttering like some frantic bird. I'd never heard anybody's heart beating before. We never thought about hearts beating in our family; we just assumed they'd go on beating. Now, listening to that heart made life seem very frail and uncertain.

But at the same time, I couldn't help noticing that she was developing bulges under her jumper like all the other girls. I'd never realised, under all those gym-tunics and loose Angora cardigans. The discovery, together with listening to her heart, put me into a very odd mood.

'I thought you'd gone for ever,' she said. 'I thought I'd just imagined you, that you were always too good to be true. I thought I was a ghost, lost a long way from home and quite unable to get back, because it was too far to walk. I was silly, wasn't I? Silly old me.'

'I'm sorry,' I said. 'But Councillor Burridge is a terrible gas-bag. She's worse than the *Shields Evening*

45

News. She'd have told *everybody*. And then my life would have been hell.'

She stroked my head in a motherly way. 'You're not very brave, are you? I mean, to be a Spitfire pilot . . .'

'Berry's worse than any Messerschmitt,' I said. 'You don't *know* him . . .' My voice came out rather muffled, because she was still pressing me against her Angora jumper.

'Make me a promise, Bob, will you?'

'Anything,' I said. It was a stupid thing to promise, but I felt very guilty, getting her into that state.

'I have this nightmare that I'm lost, and nobody will come to find me. Promise that if I ever get lost, you'll come and find me?'

'Promise.' You'll say anything to a girl, when you've upset her.

It seemed to cheer her up. She let go of me, sat up, pushed back her long red hair over her shoulder, and, wiping her eyes with her lace-edged hanky, looked at her watch.

'We'd better get going. They'll be back in half an hour.'

She seemed weary, walking home. Weary and slow. But I kept her going, with my arm around her, and it was cosy and snug. My fingers kept touching the edge of that bulge, and she didn't seem to mind. She didn't seem to mind anything, with my arm around her.

Still, I was glad to reach the green gate, and shut it behind us. And we reached the summer-house just in time. She'd hardly got her breath back from the last climb before her father was calling us for tea.

And yet all through tea she was glowing, lively as a cricket.

Chapter Five

That was the twenty-fifth of August. And you all know what happened on the third of September. Neville Chamberlain bleating over the radio that we were now in a state of war with Germany, and then the air-raid sirens went.

Us lads went mad, trying to get into the war. I mean, it went a lot further than cancelling your copy of the *Wizard* and ordering *War Illustrated* instead. More than pinning your war-map of Europe on your bedroom wall, and sticking all the little flags in it showing the position of the Nazi forces and the French and the British (and, it seemed very odd to us at the time, the Russians). More than making score-charts for the number of German ships sunk, planes shot down, tanks destroyed. We wanted to *help*.

And of course they said school was cancelled for the duration, because the schools had no air-raid shelters. And the cinemas were closed down for the same reason. There wasn't anything else to do but think about the war.

We spent the whole day on our bikes, in the lovely sunny weather, because signs of the war kept appearing overnight, and if you were the first among your mates to spot them, you were *somebody*. First there were the barrage balloons, flapping their crinkly fins all over the town, like great silver elephants. We had to run their crews down to earth, by tracing where their anchor-cables went. One in the middle of Dockwray Square; one on the edge of our own school playing-field. And the RAF blokes manning them were quite matey, and let us clean their badges and belt-buckles for them, and then we had to play football with them in the evenings, to keep them fit. (That was before the older girls began hanging around their tents; the games of football sort of dried up after that. We said bitterly that talking to girls all the time would make them unfit for the War Effort.)

Then volunteers were called for, to fill sandbags at Preston Hospital, and we got our hands all blistered, serving King and Country. And then a row of four pompom guns appeared like mushrooms overnight on the Bank Top near Nana's. And then the Anderson shelters arrived, just dumped as piles of corrugated iron in our front gardens, and we had to help our dads to dig the holes for them, and then we had to help the old age pensioners dig their holes. . . .

We worked about twelve hours a day, and loved it. Then my Dad got accepted as an air-raid warden, and I had to help him go round all the houses, sticking extra bits on the ends of gas-masks with sticky-tape, because the Nazis were inventing new gases all the time.

I won't say I never thought about Valerie; but the War Effort had to come first. All over the country, people were making sacrifices and leaving their girlfriends, to fly Spitfires, or sail destroyers on convoy duty, or intercept German raiders on the high seas. Valerie must learn to wait patiently, like all the other wives and sweethearts. . . .

And when the first fever of war had passed, and all the Anderson shelters were ready, and we did have some time on our hands, I felt myself curiously reluctant to go and see her.

I think I felt I'd gone too far; got in with her far too deep. Promises and holding hands and bulges under jumpers seemed a far-off peacetime thing now. It was simpler, less complicated to cycle round Shields and Tynemouth with Billy Brett who lived across the road, inspecting the defences and rushing home and putting them all on a map that any German spy would give his right *arm* to get his hands on (as Billy said).

And then, as grey November closed down, and it began to rain often, boredom set in. Billy and I sat on our bikes one morning, in Johnson's field at the edge of the cliffs, and had a row about a bit of barbed wire. Should we include it in our plan of the defences or not? I said it was new barbed wire. Billy said it wasn't all that new, it was showing signs of rust in places. Billy said old Johnson had put it up to stop his cattle falling over the edge of the cliff. I said that he might have done, but it would make life difficult for any German soldiers landing from the sea and trying to scale the cliff. I'm not kidding you, that row went on for two whole hours. I was pretty fed up with Billy Brett when I went home for lunch. And his invitation to cycle down the quay after lunch to look for any new armed trawlers moored there had lost all charm, so I told him to stuff his armed trawlers where they hurt most, and that was the temporary end of a lovely friendship.

When I got home, my mother started to nag me about my second-best trousers being muddy and, mad to get out of the house, I thought kindly of Valerie for the first time in two months.

My mother made me get changed into my best trousers, and clean my own shoes for once, so it was half past two before I got to Valerie's.

Her mother didn't recognise me at first, when she opened the door. She looked a bit frayed round the edges, much less glamorous in her flowered pinafore with a torn pocket. Suddenly I smelt an odd mediciny smell, and seeing Valerie abruptly ceased to be a good idea.

'She's in bed, pet,' said her mother. 'She's a bit poorly.' My feet began to edge inch by inch back towards the front gate and my bike. I hate the smell of illness, always have. And that look people get on their faces . . .

'But she'd love to see you. It'll do her the power of good. Come into the front room, while I get her put straight upstairs.'

I walked in like a condemned man, trying to encourage myself up by thinking there might be iced cakes, later, in spite of there being a war on. I read a women's magazine that Mrs Monkton had left lying on the settee. It was from before the war, and seemed as ancient as Tutankhamen's tomb. There was no fire in the grate, and the rain began to patter against the windows again. I began going over my list of British victories, to cheer myself up. The scuttling of the *Graf Spee*. The shooting down of a Dornier bomber over the Firth of Forth. A hundred German merchantmen intercepted on the high seas, on their way home. It seemed a very short list, and nearly as old as Mrs Monkton's magazine. . . .

'Hello,' said Valerie, from the shadowed doorway. 'Hello, stranger. Where have you been all my life?'

She was wearing a blue corduroy housecoat, buttoned up to her chin, that must have been her mother's. She had little fluffy slippers with pompoms on her bare white feet. Her hair was brushed back, and I could have sworn she was wearing lipstick. She looked a bit taller, somehow, and rather pale. But her bulges showed up more than usual under the housecoat, and my stomach started to go all fizzy. So I said, a bit grumpily, 'Your Mam said you were ill in bed.'

'Only a cold,' she said, 'and dying of boredom. You can give me a kiss, if you don't mind getting lipstick all over your face.'

I hesitated, and she said, 'I'll wipe the lipstick off for you, afterwards. With spit and a hanky.'

We'd just finished that when her mother bustled in with a three-bar electric fire. We were still standing up, close together, so her Mam said, 'Sit down, won't you? You make the place look untidy.'

We sat down side by side on the settee. I could still taste Valerie's lipstick.

'Won the war yet?' Valerie asked sarcastically. 'Dug your fiftieth air-raid shelter? Filled your thousandth sandbag? Finished your plan of Britain's defences, that the German spies can't wait to get their hands on?'

'How'd you know about that?'

'My spies are everywhere . . . meanwhile, I'm doing my bit as well.' She dived her hand behind a cushion, and pulled out a woollen object that seemed to go on for ever, fold after fold, like a boa-constrictor, only the edges waved in and out. 'Comforts for the troops!'

'What's that – a scarf?'

'No, it's a tank-track for a Mark Four Bren-gun carrier.'

We fell about giggling; and in the middle of the giggles, I forgave her for all the wrongs I'd done her. We were suddenly friends again. She was a good sport, was Valerie. I gave her another kiss; I was getting to quite like the taste of that lipstick.

But as soon as she had got me in a good mood, she really let me have it. She'd hardly been out of the house since the war started, because her Mam was scared of air-raids and the German bombers dropping poison gas. She was bored out of her mind. She wanted to see the barrage balloons, the pompoms on the Bank Top, the armed trawlers. Even the bit of barbed wire in Johnson's field. Really, my Dad must have done a real job talking to her Dad, about all I'd been doing.

'OK,' I said. 'I'll take you on Saturday afternoon, if it's fine. If they still go out shopping.'

'Oh, yes, they still go out shopping. More than

ever. My Mam's gone shopping-mad, since all this talk of things going on the ration.'

Funny, I thought I had it worked out. I really thought that all that was wrong with her was fussy parents and boredom.

Chapter Six

There was never a day like that last day. There was a sharp frost in the morning, that lay white till nearly eleven o'clock, melting into black patches on the pavement. I could tell, even as I walked down to her house, that there would be a frost again that night. But the sun fell on my face, warm, out of a clear blue sky; a last touch of Indian summer before winter.

Her parents had gone out. She answered the door all ready to be off. She had piled her hair up on top of her head, displaying rather delightful slim ears that I had a stupid desire to nibble. And she was wearing a new coat; a luxurious raglan in black and white tweed that looked smart and grown-up, and as warm as toast. And small pearl earrings. She looked suddenly very much a lady, and I felt shy. So I said gruffly, 'Let's be going, then!'

Everything went right, as if the old town was giving her a birthday party. When we got to the pompoms, instead of them being covered with tarpaulins like they usually were, and in the charge of one cold and bad-tempered sentry, the gun-crews were practising, shouting sharp orders and turning shiny brass wheels and revolving round and round on their bases. They saw her, and there were wolf-whistles. She didn't mind; she smiled at them shyly, and a smart young sergeant actually invited her through the barbed-wire barrier to sit on a gun and turn a wheel and whizz round, and peer through the telescopic gunsight while he held her hand to guide her. I think they, too, thought she was older than she was, though they knew she wasn't very old, and they were all really nice to her, like uncles. I suppose I should have been jealous; but it's nice when men think that your woman's a bit of all right, and we'd be gone in a few minutes, and never see any of them again, anyway.

And then I did take her down on the Fish Quay, because there were a lot of ordinary townspeople about that Saturday afternoon, men with their sons, because there was a minesweeper moored among the trawlers, a real naval ship with real gun-turrets, not just the twelve-pounder popguns that the armed trawlers carried. The people of Shields regarded the quay as a kind of cinema-substitute in those early days of the war, and word got round about what ships were lying in dock. And when the ordinary folk flocked down, the dangerous riff-raff kept indoors. Or at least they behaved themselves, and you didn't notice them so much.

The ice factory was working, and she jumped as the great blocks of gleaming ice came thundering down the tin chute; and shivered as the cold blast from the freezing-plant blew out of the open doors like a touch of the Arctic.

And then we walked past the Fish Quay sands, and the royal blue lifeboat was out on display on its slipway, and the crew were polishing her up.

And I nipped down on to the sands and got her the shoulder-blade of a codfish, bleached by the sun as white as paper, all points and graceful curves, and she gave me a kiss and put it in her pocket.

And I took her up on Collingwood's Monument, where the great Geordie admiral stood, carved in white limestone ten times the height of a man on his column, glaring out at the sea and the Germans, across the barrels of the four cannon they saved from his ship. And I told her what he said before the Battle of Trafalgar, that he wished Nelson would stop making silly signals and get on with the battle. And how after Nelson died, Collingwood stayed down off Spain, blockading the French and tending his little windowboxes full of plants sent from home. And how they sent his dogs out to him from his farm at Hexham, but all the dogs died because they couldn't take the sea. And how in the end Collingwood died, too, of old age, still at sea, still blockading the French and never came home to his farm at Hexham again.

'That's a lovely story,' she said. 'Lovely but sad.' And I think she wiped a tear away, though it could just have been her eyes watering in the wind.

I saw her give a glance towards the Priory. No, I said to myself, no tombstones today. It's much too nice a day for tombstones. So I said to distract her, 'Like to walk along the pier?'

She looked out at the pier, wistfully, doubtfully. 'How far is it?'

'A mile. Half a mile out and half a mile back. And there aren't any hills, it's flat all the way.'

She grinned and punched me on the arm. 'I can

see that. Let's go, then.' And we went, arm in arm.

The sea was rough, but not too rough. The waves were breaking against the pier, sending little showers of spray over it, like flights of white birds. But no heavier than light rain. I wouldn't have taken her, if the waves had been heavier; if there'd been any real chance of her getting wet. Besides, as we strode along, I listened to the sound of the waves. You can tell when one is going to send spray over, so you can duck down behind the granite wall and let the spray fly over your head. She soon got the hang of it; began telling *me* when a wave was going to break.

We reached the end, breathless, but only with laughing.

'This is marvellous,' she said. 'Absolutely marvellous!' She was laughing, and there was more colour on her face then I'd ever seen.

And then, to cap it all, as we stood below the lighthouse at the end, the armed trawlers began to come out, and passed us not fifty yards away. As they left the harbour, and began to pitch in the first waves, the smuts from their belching funnels fell on us, and we smelt the bacon frying for tea, in the smoke from the twisted galley chimneys, coming through the fresh salty air.

'Oh,' she said, 'life's so much fun with you. I feel I want to live for ever.'

When we started back, the wind was behind us, billowing out her coat and driving us home; it was almost like sailing.

We made it home in record time. Paused one last moment at the green gate, to admire the late slanting sunlight over the harbour. Then she took the house key from her pocket and gave it to me and said, 'Go and put the kettle on. I want to have one last *stare*.'

I walked up through the garden feeling a great content I'd never felt before. All the years ahead with Valerie. No hurrying, no pushing to get to the top. Taking our time and enjoying every bit of the way. All my life before then, I'd been thinking about the future. About 'getting on', as my mother called it. Passing the eleven-plus for grammar school. School certificate then Higher School Cert. Then university, if I could manage it. I wanted very badly to be top dog, to have nobody in a position to give me orders, to piss me about.

And since that day, I have looked back too often.

Only that one afternoon, with Valerie, I was content for it to be *now*.

The trees and ornamental bushes began to fall away behind me. Dusk was starting to deepen.

And then, through the thinning leaves and winter branches, I saw a light.

A light in their kitchen window.

I desperately didn't want to believe it. I wanted to believe that she'd left that light on by accident, before we went out. My Mam was always going on at me, for putting the light on when it was broad daylight.

But the drawing-room light was on as well. And the bedroom light, Valerie's bedroom light upstairs.

And their car was in the drive . . .

I still didn't want to believe it. We'd pulled the trick so often and never been caught. It was so *silly* to be caught now. Perhaps we could say we'd just been taking a walk round the garden . . .

And then I saw the door open, and saw Mr Monkton's figure, in his trilby hat and heavy overcoat, rising up at the top of the last flight of steps. Like a dark sun rising; like a dark ship coming up over the horizon.

He looked at me like a judge; like a hangman.

'Where is she?' he said. 'What have you done with her?'

Chapter Seven

We stood there and stared at each other. It was so unfair. I was five feet six, and at the bottom of the steps. He was over six feet, and at the top. He was a boss, and I was nothing. He had the power to give my Dad the sack. I was puny, so puny. I could never climb the stairs to where he stood. Unfair, unfair.

There was a quick patter of footsteps behind, and Valerie stood beside me; she was panting. Too much for a run up the garden. She could hardly get her breath.

'Daddy,' she managed.

'Get inside,' he said, in an awful voice.

'Daddy, it was my fault. It was my idea. I made Bob do it.'

'Get inside,' he said again.

'Not until I've made you understand,' she said. 'It was *my* idea.'

Her mother came up behind her father. 'Valerie, don't you *dare* talk to your father like that. Come up here this minute.'

That was what I could never forgive them for. All they wanted was to separate us. Like *I* was some disease she'd caught.

'Come up here, Valerie,' said her mother again. 'Or do you want me to come down there and drag

61

you up?' There it was again. They were big and strong, and we were small and weak. The grown-ups' ultimate argument. And she would do it, and Valerie would be reduced to a struggling squawking child. I don't blame her that she gave in, and slowly climbed up the stairs. What else could she do? But I knew it was the end. They'd break us apart now.

As she reached the top of the stairs, her mother grabbed her arm; the sleeve of her new coat.

'She's *soaking*,' she said. 'Soaked to the skin.' What a load of bollocks! I'd had my arm round her; she was hardly even damp from the spray, and her coat had dried on the way home. But that's the way they go on, and of course they always get away with it, being grown-ups. 'It's a hot bath and bed for you, madam! This minute!'

'Mummy, I've got to *explain*.' She struggled to loosen her arm, turn back to her father. Her mother grabbed her by main force, and dragged her away. She gave me one last despairing look over her shoulder, and was gone.

'Come in to my study,' said her father to me. 'I want a few words with you, Bickerstaffe.' Not 'Bob' any more. I was Bickerstaffe now. One of the workers who'd forgotten his place . . . I thought wildly that I didn't have to follow him into the house. I could just walk away. It was a free country. That was what we were fighting the war about.

But I went in, shaking. That was the way they trained you then. Teachers and parents and vicars. The adults were always right, however wrong. Adults were gods. And he was my Dad's boss.

He sat behind his desk, and left me standing, just like a headmaster would. And he started. They had all the power, but that wasn't enough. They had to have right on their side as well. They had to make you feel guilty.

'I take you into my house,' he said. 'I treat you like one of my family. I trust you with my daughter. And this is how you repay that trust.'

The awful guilt started to close down on me; it always does. Adults can make you feel guilty whether you are guilty or not. But part of me struggled against it; knew it wasn't the real truth. I could've said a lot; but then I thought about my Dad. So I just said, 'She asked me to take her.'

That was a mistake.

'Take her where?' he said.

'Down the Fish Quay. Along the pier. It was a nice day.'

'Down the *Fish* Quay? Along the *pier*?' Why do they always repeat everything you say, only changing the meaning? 'Do you know how *ill* she's been?'

'She seemed all right to me. She enjoyed it.'

'She-didn't-seem-ill-to-you. And what medical quali-fications have you got, *Doctor* Bickerstaffe? Do you know she's been at death's door? Do you know she's been in the sanatorium?'

That shook me. But I said doggedly, 'Nobody told *me*.'

'Those with any sense don't need telling. Do you never use your eyes?'

'She looked all right to me. She looked *smashing*.'

'She looked all right to *you*.' He raised a hand in

appeal, to no one in particular. As if the whole world was sitting in some invisible jury box to the left of him. 'I don't think you even begin to understand what damage you've done. I just hope you don't have it on your conscience for the rest of your life. Get out of my sight.' There was such disgust in his voice, such contempt. Like I was a worm. If he hadn't made me feel like that, I wouldn't have said it. But I did say it.

With my hand on the door handle I turned and shouted, 'You keep her in a cage. Like a canary. Can't you see she's bored stiff? Can't you see she wants to be *free*?'

Then, before he could reply, I walked out.

It was only on the way home that I remembered what happened to canaries that got free. All those years ago, my Nana found hers dead in a hole in the coalhouse wall, three days after it escaped.

Then I had to face up to telling my Dad. He had to know; there was no point in hiding it; his job was at stake. And I knew there was no way of breaking the bad news that was better than any other. So I just rolled in to Saturday tea, with all the home baking on the table smelling marvellous, and I told the pair of them.

My mother went as white as a sheet, and began going on like it was the end of the world. But my father said, 'Shut up, woman!' and she did.

Then my father asked me a lot of questions, over and over again. With his eyes half-closed against his fag-smoke, and his mouth set very sharp. I'd never seen that look on his face before, concerning me, and it worried me at first. And then I realised I *had* seen him look like that before.

When he came back from some union meeting, and told my mother all about it. He was always a strong union man, my father, in spite of being a foreman.

'Right,' he said in the end. 'So it was the Monktons who invited you? And he never forbade you to take his daughter for a walk? Not in so many words?'

'No,' I said. It was the truth. Just a rather special sort of truth. Trade union truth, I suppose. Like the demarcation disputes my father got so hot under the collar about.

'Right,' said my father again, as if his mind was made up. 'So now I know what to say to him, if he asks.'

'But you'll lose your job,' wailed my mother. 'After all these years.'

'Hinny,' said my father, 'they'd snap me up at Smith's Dock tomorrow. They're taking on fellers wi' one leg, they're that desperate. An' they're paying double-time on Sundays. I could make twice as much as George Monkton's givin' me.'

'But he's your friend . . .'

'Aye, Aah've been kidding meself he was. All these years. But no friend of mine talks to my bairn like that. Like he was a bit o' dirt. There's no friends in industry. Just the bosses and the workers.'

My mother began going on again. About what she should say if Mrs Monkton tackled her at the Townswomen's Guild . . .

'That's your business, hinny,' said my father. 'Now

that's *enough*. Aah'm going down the greenhouse to close the ventilators; and when Aah come back, Aah want to hear no more about it.'

He was a long time closing his ventilators. He went to his chrysanthemums for comfort, like a saint turns to prayer. While he was gone, my mother really gave it to me. I had ruined my father's life. I had ruined Valerie's life. It was the end of the world, and it was all my fault.

'I only took her for a walk! I didn't *rape* her!'

'How dare you use such language in front of your mother . . .'

I stamped off to my bedroom. It was freezing. I got under the eiderdown and tried to read Conan Doyle's *White Company*, my favourite book. It didn't work half as well as my father's chrysanths. I kept on wondering what was happening to Valerie.

I don't know what George Monkton said to my father, or what my father said back to him. My father never mentioned it; though he looked a bit grim for a few days. The main thing was, he didn't get the sack. I felt a fool for ever imagining he would. Nobody knew that gasworks like my father; he'd repaired every nut and bolt of it. And now, with the war, and the lack of spare parts, it kept breaking down. He was called out to repair it at all hours of the day and night. He said he was holding it together with tin cans and spit.

They finally built an air-raid shelter at school; under the best rugby-pitch. A great network of underground brick tunnels, with a concrete roof a foot thick. We went back to school, and tried to settle down, learning the industrial areas and products of a Poland that no longer existed. We raised a fuss about that, but the teacher said the examiners had promised to go on pretending that World War Two had never started, as nobody really knew what was going on now in Poland, and they couldn't afford to print new textbooks, even if anybody wrote one.

There were a few laughs, like air-raid practices when we all filed down the shelter, which was two inches deep in water and gave you plenty of chances to splash the others, and chuck your best mate's schoolbag in the puddles. Once, the lighting system failed, and we had a great time making ghost-screeches and grabbing the girls' knees in the dark and making them scream. Boys and girls were segregated after that.

The next best thing were the art lessons, where we did patriotic posters for National Savings all the time, which gave us a chance to draw Adolf falling on his arse, and lots of tanks and planes. All the best teachers were being called up. We got a lot of married women in exchange, and some old blokes who were a hoot, especially an Australian religious knowledge teacher called Mr Parrot, whom we renamed Mr Kookaburra. He made the mistake of asking us if we thought God existed, and we spent the rest of that term thinking up reasons why God didn't, which was a scream. And do angels have sex? I began writing and circulating fake bits of the Bible, full of 'begettings' and 'lying with a woman', and some dirty-minded idiot passed them on to the girls, with an effect we hadn't expected; which was that the girls giggled over them even more than the boys, which made the girls seem quite human and tolerable. And after that, the girls told us where the scruffy bits of the real Bible were, which we'd never even heard of; which changed our opinion of the girls yet again.

And so on to Christmas, the last Christmas with real toys in the toyshops. I got a German steam-engine, which my father didn't mind buying, because it was cut-price, being unpatriotic, and besides my father said the Germans were good engineers whatever else was wrong with them, and they didn't make rubbish like the French and Japanese.

And into the hard frost of the New Year. My parents let me go first-footing with them, for the first time, going from house to house till six in the morning, ten abreast, linking arms right across the road, to keep each other safe from the black ice. I had my first real drink, and developed a taste for home-made ginger wine (which had more of a kick than you might have imagined). And my cousin in the RAF, Young Gordon as he was always known, brought his girlfriend Lavinia, and she gave me a smacking kiss on the mouth, which was vastly approved of with cheers and laughs and clapping by the whole assembled company. And we all drank one another's health, and drank to the end of the war in 1940, and Hitler dead and peace restored.

The war wasn't going badly either, with the Royal Navy blockading the Skagerrak and Kattegat, and the RAF raiding Sylt and Borkum, and the Navy rescuing those poor sailors off the *Altmark* in a Norwegian fjord, to shouts of 'The Navy's here.'

Was I happy? I never really thought about it. I daydreamed a bit about Valerie, but the daydreams grew faded like old photographs. And the battle to do down Berry grew ever more real and earnest.

There was no sign of her; and I forgot her. I forgot the glory of our last walk, and the misery of it too. I didn't want glory, or misery. I wanted to live in the middle; like a pig in the middle.

It must have been some time in the February or March; I know it was dark at half past five. We had the blackouts up and the reading-lamp on, and the table was laid for tea, and I was doing my homework on the corner of it, while we were waiting for Dad to get home from work. Waiting for the clink of his heel-plates up the path, and the clicking of the freewheel on his bike. All through the war, that was the important noise, even more important than the news or Mr Churchill's speeches. Though of course we didn't have Mr Churchill then.

I remember Dad coming in with his black oily face, and Mam giving him a peck on the cheek, and shuddering at the taste of the gasworks for a joke, as she always did. Then she seemed to sense something in him (they were very close) and she said, 'Something's the matter!'

He shook his head, as if he was trying to shake off the trouble like a wet dog shakes off water.

'Something *is* the matter. I always know when something's bothering you . . . what is it?'

'Nowt,' he said, and went to get washed. She knew enough to bide her time. Sat him down with a newspaper under his chair, to protect the carpet from his fearsome black boots. Brought his dinner hot, under a plate, from the oven. Poured the tea, as if she hadn't a care in the world. And watched his face. We both knew he wouldn't hold out for long. He had an open happy soul, and any distress soon came bubbling to the surface.

He took three mouthfuls, then threw down his knife and fork as if they had suddenly become red hot.

'I can't tell what that feller's playing at!'

'What feller?' said Mam.

'George Monkton. First he wants my lad to play wi' his daughter, and then he turns him away an' calls him worse than muck to me. And now he's tryin' to ask him to tea wi' her again. He doesn't bloody well know what he does want.'

I gave a shiver. It was like someone had ripped an Elastoplast off a place where I'd hurt my leg. Pulling all the hairs, an' all. Valerie . . .

'Aah cannit stand a feller that's not straight wi' you,' he added. 'Sidling up to me wi' that smirk on his face, like nowt had ever happened between us. Gave us the creeps.'

I stared at him. I had no reason to love George Monkton, but sidling and smirking I could not believe of him. I got a sort of sinking feeling in my gut. If George Monkton was going on like that . . .

'How *is* Valerie?' said my mother. She must have had the same thought.

'He didn't say.' Dad looked very upset; you could tell he'd thought a lot of George Monkton at one time, and it hurt him.

'What did you tell him?' asked Mam.

'I told him the lad was too busy, what wi' the scouts an' his homework. I'm not having him playing ducks-and-drakes wi' my lad.'

Well, that settled it, then. Dad had spoken, and that was the end of it. He was *very* upset, and if I'd tried to argue, it would have thrown him into a right temper, and there'd have been a row that would have lasted till bedtime. Why should I put myself in Dad's bad books, for the sake of George Monkton? I didn't owe him a thing.

But I know now I was hiding behind an excuse. I didn't *have* to argue with Dad. I was out of the house a lot every day, and my parents seldom asked where I went. I went to the library on Saturdays, to change my library books. I went to the model-shop at Newcastle. I went to scouts. I went mooching round the blacked-out streets with Billy Brett just for laughs. I could easily slip down to Valerie's, and no one the wiser.

Until I did something wrong again, in George Monkton's eyes, and he went complaining to Dad again. You just couldn't rely on adults to keep your secret. Let alone Mrs Monkton at the Townswomen's Guild . . . and then I'd be in real trouble with *everybody*.

And yet . . . and yet . . .

Valerie. Valerie needing me. Valerie lonely and bored and miserable. I used to play with the thought in my mind, in place of daydreams, after that. Valerie thinking about me. Valerie thinking me the most important person in the world. It was beautifully sad.

But to actually go down to see her . . . the thought was scary. There was *really* something the matter with her now. She hadn't been at school for months. And I couldn't stand ill people; not in real life. Or the people who looked after ill people, and walked about with tragic looks on their faces.

So I kept her in my mind, as a romantic thought to play with. The memory of our last walk together . . . And I got on with English and Geography, and doing down Berry.

Chapter Eight

The war really started soon after that. I mean, it stopped being a weary joke, and got personal.

It happened again around teatime. Dad was a bit late, and we kept thinking we heard an aeroplane stooging around, somewhere far up above in the clouded night sky, and Mam kept pulling back the curtain a little bit to look out (but not enough to bring the air-raid wardens bawling 'Put that light out.')

She was taking one squint outside when she suddenly said, 'Look at our greenhouse,' in a funny voice that brought me up from my homework like greased lightening.

The greenhouse was on fire. Or at least it was filled with a flickering pale blue light like a sparkler on Guy Fawkes' night. I wasn't scared as much as nosy. I ran down the garden in the dark, nearly tripping over things, because the light was so blinding, and there were clouds of queer white smoke billowing over into my face, and the smell of Guy Fawkes' night.

I reached the door and looked through the glass. The whole place was full of fountaining blue sparks, springing from a centre of light so bright it burnt a hole in the middle of your eye – a round black blotch that leapt around wherever you looked. It was so weird, because the massed ranks of Dad's chrysanths still stood among the showers of sparks (though long past their best – he had his best blooms at Christmas).

But there was more than chrysanths in there – there were two hutches, one above the other, with my rabbits in them, Chinny and Biglugs. And as I watched through the glass, the front of their hutches caught fire.

I just went crazy then. Chinny and Biglugs were roasting to death and I couldn't bear it. I pushed open the greenhouse door (thank God Dad hadn't got home to lock it after shutting his ventilators) and I simply took a flying kick at the blinding white light. I felt my foot come in contact with something heavy, there was a crash of glass at the far end of the greenhouse, and then the blue fountain started up again outside, in the middle of the dying Brussels sprouts and turnips.

I turned and beat out the flames on the hutches with an old sack that was lying nearby. The flames were going out anyway. Then I felt inside the now-dark hutches with a fearful hand.

The rabbits were huddled, tight bundles of fur I could not force open, in the back corners of their hutches. But they were still alive, because they were still trembling. I pulled out Chinny and nursed her to my chest, and looked around.

The blue fire still blazed among our Brussels sprouts; there was a fine smell of roasting cabbage. The air was full of billowing clouds of white smoke, and through them here and there in the back gardens, there were other blue glares. It was just like a grand Guy Fawkes, with neighbours crashing about and shouting to each other, and cursing bloody Hitler.

And then the sirens went, and there were suddenly great flashings in the sky, and big explosions that echoed across the clouds like someone banging on a tin tray, over and over, softer and softer. And a sighing in the air. And my father suddenly appeared, and shouted, 'Get down the shelter, you little idiot, it's shrapnel.' And I shouted, 'Get Biglugs,' and we both ran to the shelter, and found my mother already there, lighting the oil-lamp, and nursing the little brown attaché case that held her National Savings Certificates, insurance policies, and a small bottle of brandy for emergencies.

That was our first experience of incendiary bombs. And sneak raiders. And how bad they were at sounding the siren in time. Dad was grateful about me saving his greenhouse. Though he shook me by the shoulders and shouted I'd been a stupid little idiot to risk my life like that, I could still tell he was grateful about the greenhouse. We had to patch the broken greenhouse windows with plywood, because there was a shortage of glass now the raids had started, and they stayed patched with plywood till the end of the war.

Mind you, we got our own back on Jerry soon after. It was a lunchtime, and I was home from school for lunch (the school dinners were far worse even than they are now – the custard was transparent and known as the Yellow Peril). Mam had just served up the rissoles and chips when the siren went, and we carried our plates down the shelter, and Mam had even gone back to make the coffee, because it was

75

quiet. I was sitting in the shelter door, watching a beetle crawling through its microscopic world, as if it didn't know there was a war on, when I heard this shouting.

Not screaming, shouting; like the shouting at a football match; excitement. Somebody in the next garden – I think it was old Tom Stokoe – shouted, 'Look, there the bugger goes – a Dornier Flying Pencil,' and I was out of that shelter before you could say 'Jack Robinson' leaving Mam squawking in my rear.

I got a lovely view of it, because it wasn't very high. Dark green on top, and pale green underneath, just like in the aero-modelling magazines. I could see the black crosses, and even the tiny blob of the pilot's head inside the cockpit canopy, and read the letters on the side, Z-KA.

It seemed to me it was flying very slowly up the river, in a dead straight line. I thought it was asking for trouble.

'Where's the bliddy guns?' shouted Tom Stokoe. 'Where's the bliddy guns? Them bliddy gunners is half asleep.' You could tell he wasn't at all scared – he just wanted them to *get* the thing, while it was there. And it *was* luscious – hanging there in the air so you felt you could almost reach up and touch it, like a grasshopper you'd caught and held in your hand.

As if the gunners had heard old Tom, there was a series of sharp bangs from down by the river. Four tiny white clouds suddenly grew in the blue sky – like instant white roses. They looked pretty and friendly, hanging there. Quite harmless. And a long way behind the German bomber . . .

'Them buggers is blind,' screamed Tom. 'Them buggers is stone blind. Get yer eyes charked, ye stupid sods!' He might have been yelling at the referee at a football match. And it *was* like a football match. You could hear people yelling all over the district; it sounded like the enemy centre-forward was heading for goal.

Four more white roses blossomed. Far too far in front this time. The whole district groaned, like the home centre-forward had missed the goal from point-blank range. And the bomber began to dwindle away up the river, towards Newcastle.

'Ye're letting him get away . . .' wailed old Tom.

And then four more roses blossomed, all in one clump, right in front of the bomber's nose. The bomber flew into the blossom . . . and did not fly out the other side. It just never came out. There was just no sign of it, except some black bits falling, that could have been anything.

I'll bet they heard the cheering in Newcastle.

I didn't cheer. I felt faintly sick. Because it had been there one minute, evil, luscious, shining with new paint. And the next minute, it wasn't there at all. It would never be there again. Four people inside it. Nazis, but still people. I suddenly realised that people could just stop existing. Just like that. There was no rule to prevent it happening. To me. To my Mam and Dad. To anybody.

Going back to school after the all-clear went (and it went just before afternoon school started, damn it, so I had no excuse for not going), I wondered whether Valerie had seen it.

At school, Berry and his lot went on so much, you'd have thought they'd shot down the bomber themselves.

My Dad said the wardens said the Army said that the bomber had been flying so slow and straight and low because it had been photographing the ships in the river and the gasworks and other military targets. My Dad reckoned we were for it (though he told me while my Mam was busy washing up, so she couldn't hear).

But nothing much happened.

Except that I got a letter, in a pretty pink envelope that smelt of perfume.

'From a lady,' said my Mam, as she handed it to me over breakfast. She was trying to tease me, trying to smile; but I could tell she was worried underneath.

We both knew it was from Valerie. I tore it open clumsily, in a panic to know what was inside.

Dear Bob,

How are you? I hear you have been playing football with incendiary bombs – I hope you scored a goal! I quite envy you all your adventures.

Would you like to come one Saturday and tell me all about them? I am better again, but *very* bored. All I have been allowed to do is knit comforts for our brave lads in France! I knitted a pair of gloves, but as one is fit for a giant, and the other only fit for

78

a dwarf, I think I'd better try and knit two more, don't you?

I'm sorry my father was so horrid to you that day. I have been working on him, to make him mend his manners. He is sorry now for the way he spoke to you – I think he was a little jealous of you! Anyway, he promises faithfully to behave himself, if you will come.

Would next Saturday be convenient? My mother has promised to bake us a cake, if you will come. She has been saving up the rations!

If you don't want to come, I shall quite understand.

Much love, Valerie.

My mother had sat down across the table, drying her hands on the tea-towel she'd been washing up with. I handed her the letter without a word. She read it, and said, without raising her head, 'I think you'll have to go. Don't you?'

'Me Dad . . .' I said, defensively.

'I'll talk to him . . . I'll make him understand.' She sounded so *firm*. And she didn't argue with Dad over many things. Normally, his word was law. She added, 'She's very lonely, I think . . .' She passed me back the letter.

I looked at it, read it again. Valerie sounded her old bossy self. Her handwriting was just the same as when I used to look in her school English book, when all the books were on the teacher's desk, and I was alone with them, lingering behind the others after school, deliberately.

Or was it a bit more shaky?

But then she'd probably written it sitting up in bed. That always made your writing shaky. . . .

'Dunno,' I said. Stubbornly. I'd got myself out of the Valerie business, and I was very reluctant to go back in. I felt I'd had a narrow escape; I didn't know from what exactly.

'You'll go,' said my mother. It wasn't an order; it was a forecast. 'You'll go because you're a kind boy, at heart.'

I went. My Dad ummed and aahed a bit, but he gave in. Then I had no choice but to put on my new trousers and the new RAF blue pullover my mother had just finished knitting for me, and, with my shoes highly polished, go and knock on Valerie's door. Spring had come again; there was stuff shoving up sharp green shoots all over their garden.

Mr Monkton opened the door to me. He shook me by the hand, and smiled, and thanked me for finding the time to come. He treated me like a little tin god. And I could see what Dad meant about his sidling and smirking. There was nothing nasty about it, but he was too eager to please. He wasn't sure of himself any more; like a big brave bully at school when somebody has suddenly landed one and knocked him on his arse.

Then Mr Monkton vanished into his study, and Mrs Monkton took me upstairs, saying, 'You've chosen a good day to come. She's fine today.'

She swung open Valerie's bedroom door, and I saw Valerie. In the mirror. In the mirror set between the two big windows of her room. She looked different in the mirror; more grown up, and oddly beautiful. I thought suddenly that the Lady of Shalott might have looked like that; and then she smiled at me, a radiant smile in the mirror.

And then swung round, on the stool set in front of the dressing-table to face me, and said, 'About time too. We almost put out a notice saying, "Welcome Home, Bob".'

(That was what people did in those days when somebody came home on leave after a long time overseas.)

I had had visions of a pale and helpless invalid. But as she stood up, I could see it was the same old Valerie. A little taller again (I hadn't seen her for months). And colour in her cheeks. And under that blue corduroy housecoat, the bulges were more prominent.

'I'll leave you in peace, then,' said her mother. 'I'll bring you up your teas on a tray, in a bit.' And bustled quickly out.

'Give us a kiss,' said Valerie, holding out her arms.

I was wary, inside. I think I knew I was again getting into something I didn't really understand. But you have to have courage when you care; like when I was saving Chinny and Biglugs. So I took a deep breath and chucked myself in with my eyes shut.

It shook me, the way she pressed herself against me. It wasn't at all sexy, in a cheap tarty movie sort of way. It just said how much she'd missed me, how lonely she'd been. She sort of warmed herself at me, like an old night-watchman on a frosty night warms himself at his brazier. I've never been wanted so much in my life, before or since. I just stayed there quite still. We were there for ages.

Then her tongue darted into my mouth, making me jump, and she pulled half-back from me, giggled, and let me go. I flopped on the bedroom sofa, out of breath. I noticed she was breathing very fast as well. With one hand pressed against her side.

She sat down next to me, by the fire. (We had fires in bedrooms in those days, when people were ill.) And she said, 'Tell me everything that's been happening. At school.'

And I had to tell her everything, even the most piffling details. Not just that Berry had said something rude to our class Amazon, Betty Wells, and Betty Wells had knocked him nearly senseless with a book, but even what book it was that Betty Wells had knocked him senseless with, and what all the teachers said about it. (They were all secretly delighted, Berry not being popular all round.) I mean, I like talking, but even I was exhausted after an hour. Still, I made her laugh a lot.

And then her mother brought up a smashing tea on a big tray, not just salmon sandwiches cut in triangles, but shop cakes and cream trifle. A feast. Valerie coaxed me into eating the lot; but I made her eat quite a lot in return, because I thought it was good for her, even though she pulled faces and played me up over it, so I had to coax her over and over again.

Her mother came to take the tray away, and glanced at Valerie's face, and then smiled at me, as if I was doing a good job. I watched her carry out the tray, with what I supposed was a silly, satisfied smirk on my face.

'Bob will have to go in a little while,' said her mother as she closed the door. 'We don't want to tire you out.'

There you go, I thought, molly-coddling her again. You *make* her feel ill, the way you go on. You don't take her out of herself.

But when I turned back to Valerie, she was sitting with her eyes half-closed. Relaxed, but half-asleep. To liven her up, I began telling her a ridiculous story about Mr Kookaburra and the stuffed stoat in the Biol Lab. But she took my hand and said, 'Don't go on so much. I'm sleepy, all warm and sleepy. Just cuddle me.'

We were silent for a bit, only listening to the crackle of the fire. And then she said, half to herself, 'I don't want to just *stop*. I've hardly started. It's not fair. I'm only fifteen. There's so many things I want to *see*.'

It was such a change in her, I didn't know what to say. I think I mumbled something about spring coming soon, and walking in the sun.

'Oh, don't start that sort of stuff. You sound just like my mother. Don't tell me *lies*.'

So I said nothing more.

She said, 'I'll never be anybody's wife. I'll never have children. It just doesn't seem *fair*. I want to live. I don't want to go down into the ground. Don't say anything, Bob. Just keep your arms round me, it's nice.'

We were silent again. Then she said, 'Would you have married me?'

83

'Yes.' What else could I have said?

'She'll be a lucky girl, the one who gets you . . .'

'Don't talk like that.'

'I have that dream every night now. That I'm lost, miles from home, and no one is coming to find me, ever. Will you come?'

The hairs rose on the back of my neck; I swear it; I felt them move against the collar of my shirt. But I said, 'Yes. I'll come.'

'Bless you,' she said, and fell asleep. And I watched her breathing, while the light in the room faded, until there was only firelight.

And then her mother came in, and switched on the light with a quick bang, and then she saw us sitting there, and she said, 'God bless you, Bob Bickerstaffe.' And I saw the tears in her eyes.

I got up to go, unloosening the grip of Valerie's hands gently. She murmured softly, in protest, but didn't waken.

'I'll come again next week,' I whispered.

'God willing,' her mother said. I walked downstairs and let myself out. I think Mr Monkton was still in his study; there was a crack of light under his door.

The next week, my father said not to go down. She wasn't well enough. But she sent her love.

And the week after. And the week after that. And I did not like the look that came over my father's face. As I said, he was not good, ever, at hiding his feelings.

And I felt relief; that I didn't have to go down there, and face that house with the smell of sickrooms, and the look on her parents' faces.

By comparison, the war was a relief; even if it was going so badly. One day we heard about the Navy laying mines in Norwegian waters, to stop the German ore-carriers creeping down under the cover of the Norwegian coast. And the next day it seemed, the Germans were into Norway, and had conquered Denmark. And then our troops were trailing back from Norway, and the Germans were into Holland and Belgium, and then we had the Miracle of Dunkirk.

And then the French surrendered.

Nobody believed it. Berry had the brilliant idea that the French were simply *pretending* to surrender, waving a white flag, and that they would open fire and mow down the Germans when they came out of their trenches. We all thought that said more about Berry than the French.

I rushed home after school, waiting hours by the radio for the next news bulletin. I remember they kept playing the *Trumpet Voluntary* by Jeremiah Clarke, to try to keep everybody's spirits up. It made me feel funny, that tune. Bitter and angry, hollow and yet brave at the same time.

When my father came in, with a very serious face, I was sure he'd heard some more bad news about the French. But he flopped into an armchair, just as he was, all dirty from work and said, 'I've got some bad news for you. Get a grip on yourself.'

I felt the grip on myself all right; it was like a vast hand squeezing my belly, and a smaller hand squeezing the back of my neck.

Then he said, 'I'm sorry, son. Your Valerie died last night.'

'God rest her soul,' said my mother, coming in with the drying-up cloth still in her hands. 'She was only fifteen, bless her.'

And then she started crying, silently, into the tea-towel, the tears just squeezing out from under her closed eyelids and dropping on the worn grey threadbare cloth.

Chapter Nine

From that moment, I seemed to be caught up in some machine of gloomy importance.

My father only said, 'She was a canny little lass. She always had a smile for you.' Then he went off to be alone in his greenhouse.

But then the female neighbours started dropping in. Had my mother heard the tragic news? I suppose it would be unfair to say they weren't upset; but they were *excited*, too. There was a lot of muttering in the kitchen, and every so often one of them would poke her head round the open kitchen door, and glance at me, where I sat by the empty fireplace, pretending to read a book. Drifts of low murmuring, with the words 'tragic' and 'tragedy' repeated over and over, and 'only fifteen' and 'how's the lad taking it?' (My mother was by this time obviously making no secret of my friendship with Valerie, but then the Monktons were considered 'posh'. I could've *killed* her.)

Finally I got sick of the rise and fall of saccharine murmurs, and pushed my way through them, and down the garden to be with Dad.

He was nipping suckers off his tomato-plants; tomatoes were his consolation in summer. The air was full of the tomatoes' sweet healthy smell. It was the smell of normality. I clung on to it.

'You can give us a hand if you like,' said Dad. 'Fill up them watering-cans and put a spoonful of Tomorite in each of them.'

I took them to the water-butt, tilted them, and let them slowly sink, like torpedoed ships at sea. At the last moment, as they filled and dived for the depths of the butt, I grabbed them and hauled them back to the life-giving air. The water was warm and pleasant on my bare arms, after the heat of the day. I spooned in the Tomorite powder, and watched it, in its turn, sink into the depths of the cans and dissolve. Then I gave the water a vigorous stir, and carried the cans back to him.

He didn't look round; it wasn't his way. He went on nipping out suckers. But he said, quite suddenly, 'Don't let them push you into anything you don't want to do!'

'What do you mean?'

'You'll see,' was all he said.

I saw all right. The next morning, my mother whirled me down to the Co-op, and paid out an astonishing amount of money for a new dark tweed overcoat for me, just like the one Dad had. I knew she couldn't afford either the money or the clothing coupons. I couldn't wear it for school; and I would soon grow out of it, I was growing so fast.

'What's it *for*?'

'For the funeral. And for paying your respects. I don't want you going down there looking like a ragamuffin . . .'

'Who says I'm going to the funeral?' It came out

like a wail. I wanted nothing further to do with that horror-filled house.

My mother looked at me, pale, with lips that trembled slightly. But there was that glint in her eye again.

'She was your *sweetheart*. You can't not go to her funeral. What would her parents say? What would everybody *think*?'

She made the idea of not going sound unmentionable. Like it would make me as bad as Quisling. Or Hitler. Outside the human race altogether.

'Me Dad says . . .'

'Don't quote your father at me. He always does the right thing. Like a *gentleman*.'

I gave in. Most Geordie lads would have done. It was another three full years before I finally stood up to my mother. I consoled myself with the hopeless thought that the funeral was three days off, and I still had three ordinary days to live before it happened.

Some hopes. That evening, after having his tea, my father went off into the bedroom to get changed. My mother, doing the washing up, was already changed, and wearing a black furry hat.

'Go and get ready, then,' said my mother.

'What for?'

'Paying your respects . . .'

'*What* respects?'

'At Valerie's. We're going down to see Valerie.'

'But she's . . .' I couldn't get out the word 'dead'.

'Don't argue. You're a big lad now. You're not a bairn any more.'

It was too late to do anything. She'd bought the overcoat now. Full of dread, I went into my cold bedroom and got changed. I put on my shining black shoes, that my mother had polished for me. I put on the rustling, new-smelling overcoat. It was comfy, and I snuggled down into it, and hated it at the same time. (I could never bear to wear it, after the funeral; I shoved it into the dark corner of the wardrobe, and two years later, my mother took it to the church jumble-sale, in aid of 'Tanks for Russia'.)

Then we all three walked down to Valerie's house, in silence. I kept saying to myself, 'We've still got Lansdowne Terrace to walk down, and Hawkey's Lane and Coach Lane.' Then there was just Coach Lane, and then just the walk along the Bank Top.

Then there was nothing left; we were standing on their front doorstep, and my Dad was knocking.

There was, I noticed looking up, a dim crack of light down the edge of the blackout curtain in one of the upstairs windows. Valerie's window. My heart sort of jumped, then sank into my guts. I wanted badly to go to the lav, but knew I would never dare to ask.

The door was opened by a middle-aged woman, a perfect stranger, dressed in black from head to foot. She said, avidly, in a low hushed voice. 'The Bickerstaffes? We've been expectin' you.'

I braced my trembling knees to walk up those dim stairs and get the unmentionable over with. Would she just seem asleep, like the dead seagull I had seen, all those years ago? Or would she be . . . I remembered the dead tom-cat in Billing's Mill.

But instead of being led upstairs, we were taken into the big lounge. There was a huge fire blazing, in spite of its being a summer night, and it got so hot I broke out into a sweat, and felt sick.

Lots of heads swivelled to look at us. There was a ring of men sitting round Mr Monkton, who sat, very quiet, looking as if he was . . . shrunk. Honestly, if he hadn't been sitting in the middle of the circle of men I wouldn't have recognised him. Except for his beard. There was a larger ring of women, dressed in black, sitting round Mrs Monkton, who looked sort of damp and soggy, and kept holding a hanky to her mouth, as if she was going to cough, but never did.

Dad went up to Mr Monkton, and shook his hand and said, 'I'm very sorry, George. I can't say how sorry I am.'

'That's all right, Jack. I know, I know,' said Mr Monkton, wearily.

Then we sat down, and there was absolutely nothing to say. We just sat in silence. Though in the other corner, the women murmured, non-stop, with the words 'tragic' and 'young' being repeated so often I felt I was going mad. My father was given a glass of whisky by the woman who had let us in, and there was an interminable discussion about whether I should be given one.

'He'd better have one,' said my Dad to settle it. 'Only a little one, though.'

I sipped it tentatively. It was bitter as hell, and burnt the skin of my throat, but it was something to hang on to; the burning bitterness of it helped.

I glanced around, surreptitiously. Most people

seemed at ease in their deep gloomy excitement. But there was one couple who seemed uncomfortable. The only pair who were sitting together, as if in self-defence. Again, strangers. But the wife shifted on her seat restlessly, and the husband kept turning his dark trilby hat round and round in his hands, as if he was measuring the brim, inch by inch.

Then the woman who had let us in, who was moving about dimly in the background like a servant, said, 'Joe and Edith! Would you like to come up and see Valerie now?'

There was a total silence. Everyone looked at the uneasy couple. Then the wife cleared her throat and said, with a desperate simper, 'I don't think so, Mrs Gleave. I think we'd like to remember Valerie as she was.'

Mrs Gleave frowned with disappointment. Everyone looked disapproving, and then turned their backs on the couple and went on with what they'd been saying or not saying before. The uneasy wife said, 'She was such a lovely girl, always laughing!' as if she was trying to get back into favour with everybody.

'She looks so lovely now,' said Mrs Gleave, coaxingly. 'Really beautiful. They've done a wonderful job with her. She just looks like she was asleep, bless her! Are you sure you wouldn't like to come up?'

'No, no,' said the wife, hurriedly. 'We'll just remember her as she was.'

Everybody relaxed again, disappointed.

I was shattered. All these grown-ups, and they were playing 'dares' like kids. Daring each other to see Valerie's body, tormenting each other with it. Using her like a bogey-man. Like that tom-cat in Billing's Mill. It made me so *angry*.

'Can we see her please?' I blurted out. I had a glimpse of my father's startled face; of my mother's, pale and shocked. I had obviously spoken out of turn. I obviously wasn't playing the game right at all.

But Mrs Gleave said, 'Of course you can, my lamb.' And opened the door into the hall.

As I went out, I heard one woman whisper, 'That's her young man,' and another whisper back, 'They take it hard, at that age. They think they're going to live for ever.'

Then I was following the woman's fat black legs upstairs, with Mam and Dad coming softly behind.

Mrs Gleave swung the door wide. Candlelight, dim and golden, shone out. I stepped in. It was like stepping into . . . eternity?

Masses and masses of flowers; the smell so strong it caught in my throat. Two candles burning, at the top end of a shiny coffin, shiny as a sideboard. The coffin-lid shoved behind the sofa we had once sat on, but its ugly shape showing, the ugliest shape in the world.

I took a deep breath, and looked inside the coffin with a sideways look, like a horse just before it shies.

White satin, lots of white satin. Some of it padded, the lining of the coffin. But she was wearing a white satin dress, like a bride wears. Her red, red hair streamed down each side of her face . . .

Mrs Gleave had been right. She did look just asleep, like the seagull had. And she was beautiful, still. Her long hands, with the sweet almond-shaped nails, highly polished. Even her bulges showed, through her dress.

I thought at any moment she would open her eyes, her marvellous eyes, and grin and say, 'What a fuss they're making. Aren't they daft?'

But she didn't. Some door was locked, that I couldn't open.

'I've never seen anyone look so lovely,' said my Mam. And there was relief in her voice.

'You must kiss her,' said my Dad to me. 'On the forehead, to say goodbye. So you know she's dead.' He bent forward, leading the way for me, as he often did, bless him. He said, very gruffly, 'Goodbye, Valerie, love. God bless you,' and stood back to make way for me.

Her forehead was as cold as a vase you put flowers in. And yet I still could not believe she wouldn't open her eyes and grin up at me, like she always did.

'Stand back for your Mam,' said my father, a little edge of worry in his voice. My Mam stepped forward and kissed her too. And then my father said, 'Thank you, Mrs Gleave.' And Mrs Gleave closed the door of the room behind us. And it was over.

I felt swimmy suddenly, going downstairs. I think my Dad just caught me in time. He must have been watching for it.

We went back into the heat of the room. Every face looked up at us avidly, seeing how we had passed the test. Somebody shoved another half-glass of whisky into my hand, slopping some over my fingers, so I had to dry them with my clean white handkerchief. We sat down, with all the rest; part of them now. We had passed the test. Unlike the uneasy couple, who I noticed had fled.

I just let the murmuring flow round me.

Valerie was dead. But what was 'dead'? Where *was* she? Was she still upstairs? Or in the room with us, invisible, listening to every pointless repetitive word that was being said? Or was she in the dark sky, or on the Bank Top, or the cliffs of the Priory, waiting for me to join her?

I remembered her fear of getting lost, and no one coming to look for her.

Maybe she was with God, like the vicar always said.

But that was the only one I couldn't believe in.

There was another knock on the door; more pale frightened faces coming in, drained of all life, as ours must have been drained.

'Time to go,' whispered my father, putting his hand on my arm. We shook hands with the Monktons again, and made our way out.

As I went out, I heard one woman whisper, almost fondly, looking at me, 'They must have been very much in love.'

We walked home in silence; and yet Dad must have been thinking of me. He said at last, as we turned in at our own gate, 'Everything has to die some day, son!'

'Aye,' I said on an indrawn breath, as he said it.

'She had a short life, but a happy one,' said my mother.

I could have hit her, for being so stupid.

Chapter Ten

I thought we would sit well back in the church, at the funeral.

But there was a murmuring in the porch, and my Dad said, 'Mr and Mrs Monkton would like you to sit with them. I think it would be a comfort to them . . .' He sounded worried, doubtful, as if he wanted to do his best for everybody, but couldn't work out what that would be.

I felt so lost, I no longer cared what happened to me. That's a bad state to get into. You can do yourself a lot of harm in that state, that you'll regret afterwards. You should always be on your guard.

So I went into the front pew, and Mr and Mrs Monkton made way for me. I looked up, and there was the shiny coffin, between the choirstalls, and it seemed to have nothing to do with Valerie at all.

I don't remember much about the service, except Mr Monkton kept giving little pointless coughs, as if he couldn't clear his throat, and Mrs Monkton cried a lot, and he kept squeezing her arm. Of the burial, I can only remember the grave-diggers standing a way off, having a quiet fag, as if they were road-menders or anything. And me picking up a handful of soil and the sound it made on the coffin-lid.

It is the funeral tea I remember. The fire burning

in the grate again, and me sweating, even though all the windows were open, letting in the summer breeze. I remember the way people looked at me, like I was one of her family now. And the whispers. Ridiculous women whispering that we had been childhood sweethearts, and that one day we had been going to marry, when we were older . . . It seemed *loony* talk . . . I'd thought grown-ups had more sense. But they don't seem to have much sense at funerals, especially women. And Mr and Mrs Monkton didn't put them straight; in fact they seemed to lap up that kind of talk, and want to believe it had been true. I suppose they were grabbing at might-have-beens, wanting Valerie to have what she never would have now . . . oh, I don't know, everybody seems to go pretty bonkers at funerals. It was just nice to get home and be quiet, because although funeral teas always start off pretty gloomy and quiet, with much knocking-back of whisky, they get a bit riotous towards the end, with everybody talking about old times and the new suit they've just bought, as if they've forgotten it's a funeral at all.

When somebody dies, you go looking for them. If it's somebody you care about. I know it sounds crazy, but you do.

I still did my school exams, but I did them in a dream. I thought I would fail the lot, I cared so little. But I still came top. Either it was because I'd done most of the work before she died, or else other people weren't concentrating either. There were a lot of distractions. Mr Churchill had just said the Battle

97

of France was over, and the Battle of Britain was about to begin. You had a sense of Hitler's armies just poised to invade, out there across the North Sea, all the way from the North Cape in Norway to the Bay of Biscay. There was a lot more evacuation, sandbag-filling, draining of flooded air-raid shelters, getting-out of gasmasks that had been gathering dust for months. I couldn't be bothered with any of it. I just went for the same walk, evening after evening, and twice at weekends. I would walk nearly to her house, to the green gate. And then along the Bank Top, down on to the quay, up on to Collingwood's Monument, across to the pier, and ending up on the Priory Cliff. Looking for her. Every time I turned a corner, my heart was in my mouth because I thought she would be there, waiting for me. That she'd grin, and wrinkle up her eyes, and say something funny and rude.

One evening, when I was on the Bank Top, there was a sneak raid. Three Junkers 88s flying in low over the North Sea from Norway, through the evening sunlight. Coming in between the piers to attack shipping. I didn't bother to take shelter, just stood in a deep doorway in the old Clifford's Fort. So I saw everything. The smoking dull-red tracer from our pompoms, curling lazily out towards the planes, and always falling behind. The planes with their bomb-doors open, and the bombs falling out, like a cow shitting in a field. The bombs all missed, as far as I could see, falling into the river making a whole wall of spoutings and spray, so you couldn't see the far bank. I think they tried to machine-gun the fat old ferry that was crossing the river at the time. They missed that, too. Then they were gone, streaking back out to sea, and then the air-raid siren went. I didn't reckon they'd done very well, for the Ever-Victorious Luftwaffe. But then our side hadn't done very well either. A few months ago, I'd have been wild with excitement, rushed home to tell Dad all about it. But now, it was just a bore. I certainly hadn't been scared for myself at all. If I felt anything, I felt invulnerable; an invulnerable ghost looking for another ghost.

Don't ever give me that crap about ghosts being scary. Nobody who's lost anybody thinks ghosts are scary. People who've lost somebody special *want* to be haunted. They beg and pray to be haunted.

And they never are. Just once I got a shock. I was walking up Front Street one Saturday afternoon for the bus, just starting to feel hungry for the first time that day, and realising again with a start that I had to eat to go on living, when I saw this girl with her back to me, looking in a shop window. A tall thin girl, with red hair streaming down her back in great thick pigtails. It *was* her. It was her ankles, her thin wrists. It couldn't *not* be her. I walked up to her . . .

She turned, and of course it wasn't Valerie at all. This one was the sort with *ginger* hair and freckles. A snub nose; eyes green as glass marbles.

'Hello.' She smiled, because I think she was a friendly girl.

I hated her, because she was not Valerie, and ran away.

* * *

My father stirred uneasily in his chair at the supper-table. Meals had been uncomfortably silent, recently. He would start talking about work, then trail off; because he couldn't talk about work for long without George Monkton coming into it.

Or my mother would go on in the usual way about how difficult the rationing was getting, but her heart wasn't really in it.

They both watched me a lot, when they thought I wasn't looking. I knew they were worried about me, and didn't know what to do about it. *I* was worried about me, when I could be bothered, which wasn't often. I couldn't think what to do about it, either. The world had broken in half, you see. One half was the war and the bombing and the rationing, all the things I should be worrying about, that I wasn't worrying about at all. The other half of the world was that Valerie was dead.

Oh, I tried telling myself that she wasn't my sister or my mother or father or anything; no relation at all, really. But she had been *mine*. I could remember, oh so clearly, her moving and breathing and sighing in my arms, more real than anybody I had ever known. And now she had been taken away for no reason at all; and I couldn't reach her any more. There was no *sense* in it. It made the whole world into a con-trick. It didn't matter how hard you worked, what exams you passed, how much you got on, how much money you made as a man, what car or house you bought. It could all be taken away from you in a twinkling of an eye, and no reason given . . .

I still went to church with my mother, dressed up in my best. Going to church was the one thing that had meaning, because there I could get my revenge on God. Oh, there were a hundred ways to insult God in church. Opening and shutting your mouth during the hymns, and making sure not one word came out. Clenching your teeth during the prayers, thinking you Bastard, you Bastard, you Conning Bastard. Thinking how stupid the vicar sounded, as he urged and threatened people into being good. What was the point of being good? People died just the same . . .

My father shifted uneasily in his seat again, then said, 'George Monkton was asking if you'd go and see them. To have tea. On Saturday afternoon . . .'

I felt a surge of pure terror. I could not bear to go down to that ghastly house again. To face the shrunken people who lived there now, people who crawled through life like half-squashed insects. . . .

'I don't think he should,' said my mother. 'The bairn's been through enough. He wants to put all that behind him now. He wants to get on with his life. You can't expect the young to live by the dead . . .'

'George is taking it very hard,' said my father. 'He's doing his work but . . .'

And suddenly, I saw a move. Like you see a move at chess or draughts. A brilliant move.

God had done the Monktons terrible, cruel, point-less damage. God was worse than Berry, who pulled the wings off flies and watched them crawl around, and laughed.

If I went, if I helped the Monktons, that would make me *better* than God.

I wanted very much to be a better person than God.

My courage nearly failed me, on the way down. My legs went slower and slower, and I hadn't the energy to keep them moving. All my life felt like it was draining away.

I came to a stop, on the Bank Top. At the end of Nana's street.

In Nana was strength. When I was little, my mother was too weak to carry me, after I was born. For a long time, Nana carried me instead. She would carry me, if I asked her, even when I was three years old. She had lost ten babies in a row, after my Dad was born. She nearly died when she was thirty-nine. All they could do for her was put a couch in the backyard when the sun shone, so she could get the benefit. And yet now, at sixty, she was built like a tank and bustled everywhere, and did the baking for the whole family, and laughed like a girl at anything that amused her. Somehow, Nana had the secret.

If she was in. I almost ran to her door. It gave to my push; she never locked it. I shouted 'Yoohoo' like all of us did, down her quiet hall, to warn her I was coming. She shouted 'Yoohoo' back, from her kitchen.

I went in. She was sitting quiet in her rocking-chair, hands in her lap. She often sat like that; she wasn't a great reader or anything. She was smiling a little to herself, as she so often did, when she was remembering people she had known. The firelight from the kitchen range, that heated her water and was never allowed to go out, shone red on the rounded curves of her face.

My father often said, in a glad voice, 'Your Nana's a strong woman,' and I saw all that strength now. She looked round and smiled, and said simply, 'Hello, hinny.' I sat down opposite. Silent. Content to be in her silence. You could be silent with her, in a way you can't be silent with anybody today. The clock ticked; her cat Mollie purred, a rounded furry cushion on the clippie rug I had helped Nana to make, when I was very small. It was enough; it was paradise.

'I'm on my way to the Monktons',' I said at last. 'To try and cheer them up.'

'Poor souls,' she said, and sighed. 'It's hard when you've only had the one.' Hard, she said. Not impossible. That was the marvellous thing. She made it sound just another mountain to be climbed, that you'd do in time.

'I don't know what to say to them,' I said.

'Say what's in your heart, hinny. What else can you say?'

'I wouldn't dare to say what's in my heart, Nana.' I was thinking how much I hated God.

'Aye, you're bitter,' she said.

I didn't have to tell her about it. She *knew*.

She said, 'I nearly died, after your grandfather died. I went all the way there, an' came back again. It's a waste of time, bein' bitter.'

'But how can you *not* be bitter?'

'There's only one thing worth learnin'. Love is stronger than the grave.'

* * *

Mr Monkton opened the door. We gave each other one startled look, eye to eye, and then both of us looked away.

'Thanks for coming, Bob,' he said, and held out his hand. I took it, and he put both his hands over my one hand. His hands were large and warm, and his grip very firm. I suddenly felt close to him.

'Tea's all ready,' he said. And there was a sumptuous spread. I shook hands with Mrs Monkton, but she wouldn't look at me at all. It made me feel very uneasy. It was hard to chew even the soft sandwiches, and I couldn't think of anything to say. Mr Monkton asked me about school, and how my parents were. And the scouts, and I answered as best I could. But the silence kept coming back. I kept looking at the fourth side of the table, where Valerie had always sat. So did they, I noticed. It grew more and more awful. They didn't mention Valerie, and I didn't dare to. I felt Mrs Monkton was going to explode, like a bomb, at any moment. Her hand shook as she poured me a second cup of tea. I had the awful feeling I would get up from that table in the end, and leave that house, and no one would have mentioned Valerie at all. And then she really would be dead for ever.

Then Mr Monkton said, gently, 'Valerie had bought you a birthday present.' He handed me a flat packet, wrapped with a ribbon in posh paper. 'When is your birthday?'

'In one month . . .'

'I think she'd have liked you to open it now . . .'

I opened it. As I did so, he said, 'We've no

idea what it is . . . she never went out of the house.'

There were two things inside. Another flat packet, and a piece of dried bracken. I'd picked the bracken from the cliffs of the Priory, and given it to her, on one of our trips.

Suddenly, she was alive again, almost in the room with us. My heart . . . I actually felt it leap for joy. Then I opened the other packet. It had a bottle of after-shave lotion and a new shiny razor. And a note in her handwriting, saying, 'For when you finally get round to shaving, he-man!'

It was a Valerie joke. It was a ridiculous present, a lovely present. It gave me her permission to go on living after she was dead.

I laughed out loud. And, amazingly, Mr Monkton laughed as well. Like a boy. He said, 'The little monkey. That was *my* after-shave, and *my* new razor. I wondered where they'd got to.'

And suddenly, Valerie seemed between us, alive and laughing and pleased at the way she had teased both of us.

'She was a terrible tease,' said Mr Monkton. 'She was always a terrible tease. Is that bit of bracken a joke as well?'

And suddenly, my tongue was released. I told him everything. All about our walks, and the things she'd said about the Fish Quay, and all the smart cracks she'd made. He laughed and laughed, as if he'd become a boy himself again, walking along the cliffs with us.

And then I told him about the last day, and the walk along the pier, and how we'd *felt*. And all the time I talked, Valerie was alive again, for both of us. And he couldn't get enough of it. We neither of us wanted it to stop. But I had to, in the end. And we both lay back in our chairs, well content.

And became slowly aware of the storm sitting beside us, about to break. We both looked at Mrs Monkton at the same moment.

She looked like a mad woman. Her face was as white as a sheet, and her eyes were like black smouldering fires. She waited a long time, then she said, 'You stupid fools. You pair of stupid male fools. That was what *killed* her, and you sit there laughing at it. She was a stupid little fool to go, and *you* were a stupid little fool to take her, and *you* are a stupid fool to sit there laughing.' Then she turned to me and said, 'You killed my daughter. Hell's too good for you . . .'

'I think you'd better be going, Bob,' said Mr Monkton hurriedly. 'Come on, I'll get your coat.' As he bustled me out of the room, she was still screaming at us. He got me out on the doorstep quickly, then paused and said, 'Don't take that to heart, old lad. She's still very upset. Thanks for coming. And thanks for telling me what you got up to.'

He shook my hand again, and closed the door. Inside, the yelling and screaming went on.

Somehow, I made it back to Nana's. Sat by the fire, shivering. Although it was July, I couldn't seem to stop.

'Did I kill her, Nana?'

She rocked a little. Then said, 'No. The day you

brought her here, her death was in her face. It was
only a matter of time. I've seen plenty go like that.'

'But you were laughing with her!'

'Can't you laugh wi' somebody, just because you
know they're going to die? We'd get precious few
laughs in this world, then. We're all going to die
some day.'

'I feel terrible about Mrs Monkton.'

'And how do you feel about Mr Monkton?'

'He *laughed*. He was *happy*.'

'You gave what you could,' she said. 'Nobody can
do more. Let's have another cup of tea. And then I'll
walk up home with you.'

Chapter Eleven

It was August 1940. I remember the placards outside the newsagent's shop, giving scores for the Battle of Britain, as if they were cricket scores.

RAF 167 NOT OUT.

I was still drifting in a dream. Drifting up from the coast, because I had no pocket-money left to spend on a bus fare.

Did Valerie first touch me then? Or was it pure chance? A small bomb-crater, outside the post office on Preston Road. Lots of glass blown in, lots of slates off roofs, and water jetting up from a fractured main making a fountain in which half-naked little boys played, till the sweating policeman drove them away.

I could either turn left, back into the town. Or turn right, past Preston Cemetery.

The town was hot and dusty and dry, and full of people who might know me. I didn't really want to meet anybody.

I turned right towards Preston Cemetery, under the green shade of the cemetery trees that overhung the road. It was suddenly cool and peaceful.

The top end of Preston Cemetery is horrible and I would never go there willingly. Just rows and rows of boring tombstones packed too tight, like false teeth.

But the old part I was passing was Victorian, and the Victorians did it better. Lots of trees and neatly mown grass verges, even in wartime, and marble angels as big as a man.

Valerie was there. I could see the place exactly, from where I was passing outside the railings. Her family must have bought a plot in Victorian times, for both her great-grandfathers were buried there. I remembered; she'd told me.

I was tired. I was tempted to go in, sit down. But what decided me was the sound of a wood-pigeon.

You see, that had been a joke between us. There had been a wood-pigeon in her father's garden at home. And she could imitate it to perfection, curling up her pink tongue, inside her open mouth. She could imitate it so perfectly that sometimes, when she left me in the garden, and went and hid from me, I would be unable to tell which call was her, summoning me, and which was the real pigeon. Once, pursuing it earnestly in the garden, I had looked up and seen her laughing and waving from her bedroom window. Doubled up with laughter.

Now, I went through the quiet gate, and followed the sound of the pigeon. If it led me exactly to her grave, I would know it was really her. That was the bargain I made. With God? With myself?

It seemed to lead me straight to her. Perhaps I cheated. I don't know . . .

VALERIE MONKTON

1925–1940

A BELOVED DAUGHTER

I sat down wearily, on the edge of the tomb next door. And told her all my troubles. Just like that old man, so long ago. I didn't feel daft, for it seemed to me she listened. Every so often, the wood-pigeon would call. And each call seemed a comment on what I was saying.

When I finally stood up, the sun was starting to set. It was cool. I remember midges were flying in clouds among the sunbeams slanting through the trees. I felt so *peaceful*. She'd listened to me; she'd answered; I was content.

'I'll come back and see you tomorrow,' I said, softly.

The wood-pigeon called again.

Chapter Twelve

I eased my bottom on the tomb next door. Even in summer, the cold struck up, after a while. It was bearable, if you sat first on the left cheek of your bum, then the right.

'The Spitfires are knocking down an awful lot of Jerries,' I said to Valerie. 'A hundred and twenty-eight, yesterday, they said on the news. For the loss of thirty-four of ours, and nineteen of our pilots saved, by coming down by parachute.'

There was no response of any sort. But then, I thought with a sigh, she'd never really been interested in the war. And it wasn't an interesting sort of day. The clouds were solid grey cotton wool, resting on your head. The trees were the dull dark green of August, and the white angels shimmered at me through the gloom. It was muggy; it was hard to concentrate on anything. But I noticed the flowers on her grave were still changed every day. Her Mam must do it. I glanced up the gloomy vistas of the graveyard uneasily; I had no desire to encounter her Mam, after the last time. She'd probably accuse me of trying to steal the flowers off the grave . . .

'Me Dad bought me Mam a new pair of suede boots,' I told Valerie. 'For the winter. They're bright green, and she hates green. She'd rather have had brown. Me Dad could have got brown, but he likes bonny colours. She damn near threw the boots at him. And he can't change them either, because he bought them off a feller at work. They were off the Black Market.'

Some distance off, the wood-pigeon sounded, a bit sarky, but amused. At least I wasn't being a total bore. It was hard to think up new things to tell her, every day. And, talker though I was, nobody likes doing a monologue for ever, even with pigeon-coos.

'The Mayor's resigned, it said in the paper. Using petrol meant for official purposes in his own car, illegally. They say he'll get six months . . .'

I broke off, because there was a noise overhead. Above the clouds. A noise like a lad running a stick along a row of metal railings. I knew that sound. It meant there was an air-battle starting up overhead, and they hadn't got round to sounding the air-raid siren again.

I got up quick. Life had gone back to normal a bit, since I'd tracked down Valerie. Normal enough for me to dislike getting killed by falling shrapnel. Though the guns wouldn't be firing just yet, because our fighters must be up there. Still, even spent machine-gun bullets dropping were enough to kill you; they flattened themselves when they hit the roads, into little silver mushrooms. God knows what they'd do if they hit you on the head.

None of the trees around me looked solid enough to stop a bullet, so I ran for the cemetery gates. There was a big air-raid shelter at Preston Colliery, just up the road. Or some householder might have mercy on me and call me into their Anderson. I shouted 'Ta-ra' back to Valerie. I never like to be rude.

I had reached the gates when it happened. There was suddenly a dark blob in the clouds ahead, and then it solidified into a plane diving straight at me. A Jerry, because it had two engines. I ducked behind the cemetery gatepost, because it was coming in low, and those guys shot at anything that moved. They even shot at fishermen they caught fishing. They didn't seem to know the rules about military targets. . . .

It came down so low, before it straightened out, that you could see the pilot's face. And the front gunner's. But they weren't after me. Somebody was after them. Because two single-engined jobs came out of the same hole in the clouds, one after the other. Hurricances. My Dad said the Spitfires knocked them down, and the Hurricanes chewed them up. Seemed logical. Hurricanes were fat, like Heinkels, and not so fast as Spitfires.

It was quite a do after that. The Heinkel was mad to get away out to sea; but the Hurricanes cut it off and turned it back. They chased it all over the shop. You could see the little flashes of the guns along their wings, and the long trails of soot that firing their guns left. They were very determined, but they didn't seem to be very good shots. Bits would fly off the Heinkel, but not very big bits, and in unimportant places, like the outer wings and the tip of the tail. The Jerry pilot could certainly fly; he kept twisting and turning like a rabbit does, when a dog's after it.

It got a bit agonising in the end. I actually got to feeling sorry for the Jerry. It must have felt like

113

being mauled to death by old dogs with false teeth.

And then, the next time they came over, one Hurricane got him in the port engine. A long white plume of glycol smoke came trailing out. And at the same time, his wheels dropped down, and his bomb-doors opened. And black things began falling out . . .

Right over my head.

Bombs.

I flung myself into the nearest flower-bed. I remember it was full of big fat marigolds. I just lay there envying the big fat marigolds, because they would go on living even if they were blown in half. And I wouldn't.

I never heard a sound. I didn't hear anything for three days after, and they thought at first I would never hear anything ever again. I know blood came out of my ears, because they had to wash it off when I got to the hospital.

But I felt a lot. It was like a storm of wind, trying to pick me up, dragging me along the ground, so I clung on, digging in my toes and fingers and expecting to go flying up in the air at any moment.

Then the flower-bed kicked me in the chin, making me bite my tongue. It kicked me in the gut, knocking all the breath out of me. It kicked me in the knees, making my feet fly up in the air behind me.

And then, as if that wasn't enough, the wind reversed, and tried to drag me back towards the bombs . . .

I waited till the last funny thing had happened, and

114

then I got up slowly, feeling myself all over, and looked where the bombs had dropped.

The cemetery looked like one of those paintings of the Western Front in World War One, that they show you at school on Armistice Day.

All the leaves were off the trees. So were most of the branches. There were just jagged stumps, and bomb-craters. There was a half-tombstone, a black marble job, lying just in front of me. Split down the middle.

IN LOVING MEM
JOSIAH LIVI
BELOVED FA
PASSED AW
12 DECEM

Another two feet and it would've squashed me flat.

And there were bits of smashed white bone lying round it. And queer drooping objects hanging on the shattered branches of the trees; I couldn't make out what they were at all.

I could still see the big white angel that had belonged to Valerie's grandfather. It was leaning over the edge of a crater thirty feet across, with no arms left and no head.

Where Valerie had been, there was just a great big hole, filling up with water.

Two wardens ran up then, and shouted at me, and I couldn't hear a thing; like a silent movie.

They led me away to Preston Hospital.

I read about that raid. In the newspaper Dad

brought me in hospital. It had been a bad raid for the Jerries. They'd lost eight Heinkels, six Messerschmitts and five Junkers 88s. None of our planes was shot down. Nobody else was hurt, except me.

And Valerie.

The first faint words my mother said to me, that I heard, were, 'What were you doin' down Preston Cemetery?'

'Seeing Valerie.'

'That's morbid,' she said. 'That's morbid at your age. You're not to go down there again.'

'No point,' I said. 'Valerie's gone. Do the Monktons know, Dad?'

'Aye.' He sighed, on an indrawn breath. 'They've taken it very hard. It's like she's died again, to them. They've nowhere even to put flowers any more. They gave George a month off work, he's so shook up. They've gone down to her mother's in Cornwall. There's a replacement manager coming in every day from Howdon. A young twit who doesn't know his job.'

Even in the depths of my misery, I spared a pang of sympathy for the young twit who didn't know his job.

'If you pass their tests,' said my mother, 'they'll let you come home tomorrow.'

The tests seemed to consist of an elderly doctor who came into my part of the ward and stood in the corner with his head upside down, muttering things like 'Ninety-nine' and 'Forty-four.'

I yelled 'Ninety-nine' and 'Forty-four' back to him,

covering first my right ear with my hand, and then my left. He wrote something down on his clipboard and went away again, leaving me to think about life. In tentative stabs, like your tongue stabs at an aching tooth.

I should have been glad that that Heinkel had crash-landed on the sands near St Mary's Island, and all the crew walked away unhurt. I should have been glad that neither of the Hurricanes was shot down. I should have been glad he dropped his bombs on the cemetery, and not on living people in their houses.

I wasn't glad. I could not manage to be glad about anything. It was terrible to bomb people after they were dead; to bomb their underground world. They deserved to rest in peace. It was like Hitler was bombing Heaven. Bombing God. There was nowhere you could escape to, even when you were dead.

Everybody was upset about that bombing. My Nana said that unless the body was properly buried, the dead couldn't rest, but would have to wander round the earth . . .

Next day, I was sent home, and just lay about all day on the couch, stroking our dog. It drove my Mam nuts. She couldn't bear people moping, she said. It drove her into a frenzy of house-cleaning. I think she would have liked to have thrown me out with the rest of the old rubbish. She kept on bringing me all my old toys, and asking if I still needed them. They could go to the children of people who had been bombed out. (I am sure she was doing it just to annoy me.) After lunch, she started on my clothes. This was too small for me now, that was too small for me . . .

I just grunted at her, till she brought out my green suede jerkin. 'This is too small for you, too. You haven't worn it for ages . . .'

'Give me that!' I grabbed it off her. It was the jerkin that I'd worn a lot when I used to take Valerie for walks. I wouldn't have parted with it, if it had been small enough to wrap round Chinny and Biglugs. I sort of hugged it to me.

'Well are there any dirty hankies in the pocket, then?'

I groped. But all there was was a small round hole, in the bottom of the left hand pocket. And, below it, something in the lining of the jerkin. What could it be? I groped.

It was a door-key. And not for our front door, either. Whose, then? How could it possibly have got there?

And then I remembered. Remembered Valerie giving it to me that last glorious day, and saying so clearly, 'Go and put the kettle on. I want to have one last *stare*.' Giving me the key to their front door.

And in the row that followed, we'd all forgotten it. Valerie, me, even Mr and Mrs Monkton. It must have been Valerie's own front door key, from when she was younger, and not ill, and went out to school like any other kid. She was ill all the time after that, and they'd never missed it.

Valerie's words seemed to go on ringing inside my head. Bright, bossy, full of happiness.

'Go and put the kettle on.'

This was no accident. This was a sign. Like the

wood-pigeon. She had led me to find the key. She wanted to see me. It was all going to be all right. It was her way of telling me it was going to be all right. I was so happy, I nearly leapt up and embraced my mother. I only just remembered to sit still in time.

'What's that you've got?' asked my mother sharply.

'It's an old key,' I said.

'Where to?'

I realised that I would lie to her till the cows came home, as far as this key was concerned.

'It's the latest craze at school. Collecting old keys. I swapped it for an army badge . . .'

'And a right bad bargain you got – useless rubbish!'

But I got away with it. We were all great collectors then – cigarette cards, matchbox covers, old battered soldiers, Dinky Toys, shrapnel, cartridge cases. You name it, we collected it.

'Pity you haven't got anything better to do,' said my mother.

I hardly heard her, I was so full of joy.

Valerie had sent for me. As my Nana said, love was stronger than the grave. She had been taken from me by a Great Bully, and she had escaped the Bully and come back to me.

What I have told you before, you probably found easy to believe. Because you've seen Spitfires and Heinkels and air-raid wardens in books.

The next part you may find a bit harder.

Chapter Thirteen

It was a smashing evening, the evening I walked down to Valerie's house. The sky was high and clear and blue; the birds were still singing; the barrage balloons floating low, nudging at their wires like impatient cows. So low, you could see the little breeze making wrinkles on their fins, like little waves running across a silver beach. The balloons flying low meant there would be no raid this evening.

The houses glowed in the sun; even the bombed houses and warehouses looked old and far away, like antique ruins as ancient as Julius Caesar. There were a lot of people about, their faces tired, but glad with the sun. But they seemed far away from me too; because I was going to a different world. I was going to meet Valerie, somewhere beyond space and time. I felt like an RAF pilot, going on a dangerous but exciting mission. My mind was careful, but my heart was thumping.

I took a wary look round, before I turned in at her gate. People were still nosy in Shields, in spite of the bombing and the weariness. If anybody saw me, who knew my Dad or Nana . . .

But there was nobody about. Everything was going my way. I slipped through the gate, closed it carefully. The moment I was in the garden, the wall and the bushes and little trees hid me from the road. I was in Valerie's world. Every bush and tree seemed to say hello to me, welcome back. Already, I could feel she was there.

I had a momentary panic that the key wouldn't fit. But it slid in and turned without bother. The smell of the house came out to greet me like a cat; the smell of her Dad's pipe, her mother's eau-de-cologne. But they were faded, cold, nothing. Her Mam and Dad were not there. There was just me and Valerie.

I stood and listened. There was only the ticking of the grandfather clock in the hall.

I called.

'Valerie? I'm here! I've come!'

Only silence. But not a cold empty silence; a waiting, holding-your-breath silence. I knew she was playing hide-and-seek with me. That would be the way she would do it. She'd always loved hide-and-seek, when she was alive. Among the bushes in the garden. Even in the house, when her parents left us alone, she would suddenly vanish, and I would have to search for her, increasingly anxious, and then find her hiding behind the kitchen door, gripping her white lace-edged hanky between her teeth to stop herself giggling and giving herself away.

'All right,' I called. 'Hide-and-seek it is, then. Off, coming away!' That was what we always called, when we started playing hide-and-seek.

I burst through door after door, expecting to see her behind each one; my heart pounding, my whole body braced for the impact. Nothing, except the empty sitting-room, the empty kitchen. And yet each

121

contained some thing of hers. In the sitting-room, her favourite picture of the Farne Islands; in the kitchen, the egg-cup shaped like a yellow chicken that she always had her boiled eggs in. And each time I plunged into a room and found it empty, there was a sense of giggle in the air, as if she had just vanished from it, and was laughing at my disappointment.

Oh, I knew now that I wouldn't find her downstairs. She would play out the game till she had wrung the last drop of amusement from it. She would be in the last room I looked, whichever that was.

So I left her bedroom till last. I went into her parents' bedroom, pointlessly, *not* expecting her; feeling like a thief, a snooper. In a funny way, the ghosts of her parents were in their bedroom; sad, bitter, angry ghosts. Mr Monkton was there in the big old tartan dressing-gown, hanging on the back of the door. Mrs Monkton was there, in the array of lipsticks on the dressing-table, and a silky thing I didn't look at too closely, tossed down rumpled on the bed. It was funny that people could leave their ghosts behind, even when they were still alive . . . But they were small, weak ghosts I could easily ignore.

In the two spare bedrooms, there weren't any ghosts at all. Spare bedrooms are cold soulless places, full of old suitcases and disused ironing-boards, piles of spare curtains and cardboard boxes. And the loo was just the loo. Though the moment I saw it, I realised I wanted a pee, badly. The sound of the flushing, the cistern refilling, were like unwelcome intruders, blocking off the first faint sound I might hear of Valerie.

122

I looked into the bathroom without hope; but there were still three toothbrushes in the chromium rack screwed above the basin. I wondered which had been hers. The red one, the blue one, or the green one?

That left only her bedroom. It was almost too much for me. My heart was pounding like one of my Dad's great steam-engines at the gasworks. I had to take it gently. I turned the door-handle, and held the door open six inches and listened. The smell of Valerie came out to meet me; the delicate ladylike smell of her perfume. Lily of the Valley, I think it was. And something more came out. You know how, when you go into a room, you can always tell if somebody's in it or not, even if they don't make a sound? I don't know how you do it. But I *knew* there was somebody in that room, waiting, breath held in, waiting to jump out on me. I thought my heart was going to stop. It would be like . . . when you were wading in the sea, and a great big breaker came in and hit you. Without warning, with terrible force, with a wave of icy cold whooshing up your front that paralyses you so you can't even breathe.

Seeing Valerie would be like that.

I pushed the door open wide.

The room was quite empty. Everything was exactly as it had been when she was alive. There was even a vase of her favourite freesias on her dressing-table, between the two big windows. Their smell mingled with all the other smells that were Valerie. Her bed was turned down, her nightdress lay ready for her to put on, just as her mother had left it in life.

But . . . nothing else. The room seemed grey and dim; inside my terrible shock of disappointment, I thought that somewhere near the horizon, the sun must have gone behind a cloud . . .

'Oh, *Valerie*,' I said, like a child who hasn't got a present on Christmas morning. The hateful dullness of a world without her came down on me like a lead weight. It was unendurable that she should not be. What was the point of going on at all?

And then, out on the horizon, beyond the spires and chimneys of the town, beyond the distant line of the Cheviot Hills, the sun came out from behind its cloud again, like a round red eye. And the whole room lit up with a strange dim red light, that I had never seen before in my life. It lay on the wall above the fireplace in horizontal bars, showing the shadows of the leaves of the trees in the garden, drawn out into long elongated shapes like claws and witches' faces. Shapes so odd they blew my mind wide open. Suddenly, I knew that *anything* could happen, that the rules of my world, of my life, could change into something I had never even dreamed about.

And I knew she was there, behind me.

But if I turned, she would be gone.

I just stood and stood and stood, as the icy fingers of gooseflesh ran up and down my spine. It was like when you tickle trout. You put your open hand in the water, and you slowly feel the trout moving in between your splayed fingers, you feel the tiny movements of its fins reaching you through the water.

But you know that if you close your fingers too

124

quickly, try and snatch, it will be gone, and your fingers will close on nothing.

I did not dare move, for fear she would be gone and leave me empty for ever.

But there must be more than this . . .

That is the way of lovers; always they want more than they've got.

Then the thought came into my mind.

Sit in the chair at the dressing-table. As she had once sat. Look in the mirror. As she had once looked.

I pulled out the chair; the legs dragged on the carpet. I sat down gingerly.

I looked in the mirror, and saw my own face, my eyes staring with the white showing all round; the mouth open, showing my teeth.

And then I looked beyond my own face.

And she was there, standing back in the shadows of the room. Grinning at me; with that sarky look of triumph on her face.

My heart froze for a long moment; and then kicked like a mule.

And her words came. I know they did not come through my ears. I know nobody else would have heard them, if they'd been there. The words were just suddenly there in my mind; I never even felt them come. I know they didn't come one by one, like when somebody speaks normally. They were all suddenly in my mind together. And yet they had a ring, as if she'd really spoken them.

'You took your time . . .'

'I'm sorry,' I said. 'I came as quickly as I could. My

Mam's kept giving me jobs to do all day. I couldn't get away till after tea . . .'

'I'll believe you,' she said. 'Thousands wouldn't.'

'Can you come a bit closer?' I said. Her face in the mirror was very small and dim and far away. And always a lover wants more.

She swam up towards me in the mirror, still grinning. 'Are you sure you want me to? Sure you're not *scared*, Bob Bickerstaffe? After all, I am *dead*. You saw me dead. All dead and beautiful. Looking just like I was asleep.' Her voice was mocking. Not mocking me, but that woman who had been in charge at the funeral.

I gave a slightly nervous snigger, and she grinned more broadly, in the mirror. 'Is that close enough for you?'

It was nice she could still be flirty. I looked at her face a long time. What the soppy books called 'feasting my eyes'. She was as beautiful as ever. The red hair was just as thick and luxurious, coiling down the chest of her white lace nightdress. She still had her bulges, under the lace. Her eyes were just as huge and as shining. Her lips parted, showing just a hint of her upper teeth. There was colour in her cheeks. I took a long, long look at every bit of her I could see.

'Have you seen enough?' she asked at last. 'I'm not your private property, you know.'

'Can you . . . touch me?' I was still scared that this might be a dream. I'd dreamt about her a lot since she died. Often, I'd seen her, and always I said, in my dream, 'There you are. Where've you been hiding? You're supposed to be dead.' And

126

always she'd grinned and said, 'Of course I'm not dead, stupid.' And then immediately vanished.

She pretended to think now, her head on one side, like she always did. 'I'm not sure I should. It mightn't be good for you. You mightn't like it. I'm very *cold*, you know. Are you sure you want me to?'

'Yes,' I said, very definitely. Feeling wasn't dreaming. Feeling was *real*.

Her face was full of mischief; the tip of her tongue peeping from the corner of her mouth, she raised one finger, one long pale finger with its burnished nail, and touched my shoulder.

Her finger was like ice. Colder than ice. The cold spread across my shoulder-blade and crawled down my spine like a long worm. I gave a great shudder, and she laughed and lifted her finger off again.

'I did warn you. You mustn't encourage me. I like it. You get my cold, and I get your warm. I haven't had any warm since I died. You are so very nice and warm, Bob Bickerstaffe.'

And her eyes did look warmer; she looked very pleased with me, like when I'd cuddled her, when she was alive. She said, 'I'm very fond of you, Bob Bickerstaffe. You kept your promise.'

'What promise?'

'That if I was ever lost, you'd come and find me. I've been so . . . lonely.' The smile had gone from her face in the mirror. Her huge eyes were suddenly dark and bleak.

'But I came to talk to you in the cemetery . . .'

'Why on earth did you think I'd be at the cemetery?

127

Nasty horrible place. I always hated it. I came straight back here. Why did you think I was in the cemetery?

I was at a loss for words. Then I said feebly, 'I heard a wood-pigeon calling.'

'What a booby you are. The world's full of wood-pigeons calling. Why did you think I'd turned into a wood-pigeon, for heaven's sake?'

I shook my head in numb misery.

'Sorry,' she said. 'I didn't mean to get narky with you. But I've been so lonely. It's terrible, being that lonely.'

'Didn't it help being with your Mam and Dad?'

'They didn't even guess I was here. When I died . . . everything was getting grey and going away. Dad was cuddling me, but he was fading away, too. He was shouting at me to speak to him, but his voice was getting fainter and fainter. And I couldn't see any more. All I could feel was the sheets between my fingers. I was hanging on to the sheets between my fingers, because they were the last thing in the world. And then suddenly I felt fine. I could see again, I could move again. I saw the two of them standing at the end of my bed, cuddling each other and crying. And I jumped up, shouting I was all right again.

'And they just took no notice of me. As if they couldn't hear me. And I grabbed Daddy's shoulder. And my hand went straight through him. And then I looked back and saw myself still lying in bed. And then I knew I was dead. It was horrible. And all the time after that, I was trying to get their attention. And they were just blind and deaf, and wrapped up in their own misery. I even found I could do little things, like making postcards fall off the mantelpiece. But they just took no notice. Any of them. I could tell all that they were feeling. Daddy was just a great lump of frozen misery. But Mummy hates me half the time, for making her so miserable. For being a failure. For not being *well*, like other girls. She's ashamed she gave birth to me . . .'

I was so sorry for her I forgot that she was dead. I leapt up and turned round to cuddle her.

And there was nothing there. Nothing but the smells of her bedroom. The sun was gone altogether now; it was growing dusk. Shadows were thickening in the corners of the room. And the room was so cold. Biting cold, piercing cold. It might as well have been a January of deep frost, instead of August. And I began to shiver uncontrollably. My teeth were chattering.

And I knew she wouldn't come back tonight. I didn't even want her to come back tonight.

I said, 'Goodnight, Valerie. I'll come back and see you tomorrow.' Then I staggered downstairs and let myself out.

The summer evening air was like a warm bath on my face and hands, all the way home. And yet I had hardly stopped shivering by the time I got to my own back door.

Chapter Fourteen

When I woke up next morning, I didn't believe any of it had happened. It had been just another dream, more vivid than the rest. I *wanted* to believe it hadn't happened. The memory of the cold in that house, the coldness of her finger . . . I didn't want any more of that. I suddenly had a great appetite for things that were real. Like my mother, and breakfast, and the morning paper, and going and picking fresh dandelions from round the edge of the school playing-field, for Chinny and Biglugs. They all seemed such blessed, honest things, that drove away the memory of darkness and cold.

That lasted until halfway through the afternoon. Then I suddenly got bored with all the realness again, especially as my mother nagged me to clean out the rabbits' hutches, until we had a row about it. In the middle of cleaning out the hutches, a wicked flicker of excitement tickled in my tum. I wanted another shot of darkness and cold, really, I suppose. But I sold myself the idea that I was just checking up on things. I mean, either it had been true or it hadn't. It teased my mind, and I had to settle it, once and for all.

By the time I got to Valerie's garden gate, I was

shivering with excitement. The silence and loneliness of the garden, the sounds of the world outside fading and growing dim, the sliding of my key into her lock, the feeling of being master of the house, conqueror of all the loneliness. I am he who comes, I told myself in a melodramatic way.

Straight up the stairs. I wasn't inclined to mess around with Valerie's little games a second time. I would summon her and she would come; or else I would go away and forget her, and then it was she who would be sorry.

I sat straight down at her dressing-table, feeling the total expert in such matters.

'Valerie!'

No reply. All right, play your silly little games with me, madam. We'll see who'll win. . . .

'C'mon out, Valerie. I know you're there. Stop being such a kid.'

Still no reply. I had an impulse to start opening the drawers of her dressing-table. She couldn't stop me. I opened the top drawer. Lace-edged hankies and little bottles of scent. The next drawer down was frothing with forbidden femininity; silk and lace. I didn't touch it. But I wondered whether she'd kept a diary; written things about me in it. . . .

I never found out, that time, because she said quite clearly, just behind me, 'Naughty. Oh, naughty.'

I nearly jumped out of my skin. Flicked a terrified glance into the mirror, and she was grinning down over my shoulder.

'You really think you own me now, don't you?'

I laughed, uneasily.

'Close those drawers this *minute.*'

I closed them.

'I think you're *horrible.* You were looking for my diary, weren't you?'

'I wanted to find out what you'd written in it about *me.*'

'Oh, yes, *me, me, me.* That's all you alive people ever think about. *Me, me, me.* That's all Daddy ever thinks about, these days. And Mummy. They keep on saying to themselves, poor little me. Why did it have to happen to me? Daddy blames Mummy because I was born sickly, and Mummy blames Daddy. I really enjoy it, when they sit brooding for hours over things like that.'

'If I'm so horrible,' I said, 'I'll go away.'

She was silent. I glanced at her, again, in the mirror, cocky, sure I'd made my point. Her grin had gone; her face looked so bleak it was unbearable.

'I've spent a whole night alone, in the dark and cold,' she said. 'And then you come and bully me.'

'Oh Valerie,' I said. 'I'm only teasing you. Don't be so solemn.'

'Solemn,' she said. 'Solemn? Wait till it happens to *you.*'

'Oh, I don't know,' I said. 'I might enjoy it. Being able to walk through doors and walls. Being able to go anywhere and nobody can see you. Appearing and disappearing and frightening people out of their wits. I'd haunt Berry, I think. Haunt him something wicked. Until he apologised for everything he'd ever done to me. Until he *crawled.*'

132

'You don't *understand*,' she said. 'You don't understand what it's like at all. It's not fun to do things like that. It makes you feel not real. Like you don't really exist. Like the merest draught under the door could blow you away. You just don't know how lucky you are, being solid. And warm. Having a body to live inside. You can curl up inside your nice warm body and fall asleep all night. Safe. All I can do is wander about. And it doesn't matter where I go, because every place feels the same. Cold. Cold. Cold.'

'Do you want to touch me? Do you want some warm?'

'Don't you mind?' I'll give her that. She sounded doubtful, worried. Then.

'Go ahead,' I said. Like I was a millionaire, with all the money in the world.

I felt the pressure of her long slim hand on my shoulder. The shiver went right down into my feet, I swear it. I felt all the warmth was being sucked out of me. But I bore it, for her sake. And I looked at her in the mirror, and saw the colour come back into her cheeks, and the smile to her face. I felt proud, that I could do that for her. I felt like somebody saving somebody else's life with a blood transfusion. I felt like a mother, feeding a child.

After a long while, she said, 'That's enough for now. Thanks a lot.' Her hand went away.

I couldn't speak, I was shivering so much.

'Now I've made you cold,' she said. 'You look awful. Why don't you go downstairs and make yourself a cup of tea? And there's plenty of cake in the tins. You can have a feast.'

133

Her face in the mirror was so full of concern for me, so full of . . . that look made me feel so *special*, like I was the most important person in the world. It was worth all the pain of the cold.

'I will,' I said, 'if you'll come with me. I don't want to leave you, even for a minute.' I felt very possessive.

'All right,' she said, after a pause. 'But you mustn't look at me. Not yet. I'm not strong enough to be looked at, yet. Only in the mirror. I'll just disappear if you look at me. When you look at me like that, I feel you want to *eat* me; even in the mirror.'

'OK.' I got to my feet with an effort.

'I'll walk behind you, so you're not tempted.'

We had a fit of the giggles in the kitchen, because I didn't know where anything was. And besides, the Monktons had turned off the gas, electricity and water when they left. But she told me where to find things, and I kept feeling little tiny gentle touches of her hand on mine. Not enough to make me any colder, just touches that made my skin prickle with delight.

So after about an hour, with the help of the bowl-shaped electric fire from her father's study, and a lot of very nice currant-cake, not at all stale yet, I got warm again.

'We'll have to look after you,' she said maternally. 'We'll have to keep your strength up.'

But still the whole house felt cold. It was weird, feeling shivery, yet looking out of the window at the deep blue sky, and the thick yellow sunlight lying on everything, and even a shimmer of heat over the crazy paving round the bird-bath.

'Let's go for a walk,' I said. 'Like we used to.'

I heard her sharply indrawn breath.

'C'mon. Just round the garden.'

'All right,' she said, reluctantly.

'I'll get really *hot* in the garden. Then you can touch me and cool me down, if you like.'

It was marvellous to step out into the heat and light of the garden, after that cold house. It was marvellous to break out into a sweat that made the increasing touches of her hands on the back of my neck and arms exquisite, like fluttering icy butterflies.

Finally, we sat on our same old seat.

'I'm so happy with you,' she said. 'Happier than I've ever been. You are nice to me, really.'

'Am I? I thought you were scared I'd eat you up with my eyes?'

'I wouldn't mind being eaten by you. It'd be nice and snug, inside your tum. Like being a baby again. I can remember being a baby so well – before I was born. It seems such a happy time, now. I think I must have hated being born.'

'Show yourself,' I said. 'Let me see you without a mirror. Let me eat you up with my terrible eyes!'

'I'll try. Look the other way, for a minute.'

I looked out over the harbour. At the waves up-river twinkling through the heat haze, and the smoke from the shipyards. There was the rattle of riveters from the dry-dock. A tug whooped commandingly, imperiously, at the huge oil tanker it was leading out of the harbour. I think the east coast convoy must have been coming out then, for there were

135

other blue shapes manoeuvring behind the tanker. I noticed all that, though my heart was pounding with excitement.

Then she said, 'You can look now. You can eat me with your eyes.'

She sat beside me on the seat, wearing a summer dress I remembered well. Smiling that smile, her face full of colour. It was as if nothing bad had ever happened to us. It was as if we had remade the world, as it used to be. I remembered my Nana saying, 'Love is stronger than the grave,' as I reached out to put my arms around her.

Her eyes flared with alarm. 'No,' she said. 'No.' But my arms were round her by that time.

She was not a shape of weight; she was a shape of cold, exquisite cold. A cold I suddenly wanted.

Then the world went dark.

When I came round, I was alone in the garden. I could hardly lift my hand to my face. Either my hand was numb or my face was numb. I felt odder than I'd ever felt. The sun was still hot on my skin, but it wasn't getting through to the cold underneath. I just sat. I heard Christ Church clock chime five, quarter past, half past, and I could not move. I felt the world was tearing past me, and I couldn't move to catch up.

Only at quarter to six was I able to stand up and walk. Like an old gaffer. I made sure I had the key, then I closed the front door, and set off for home. It wasn't much of a hill, up to home, but it felt like Everest.

When I walked into the house, my mother took one

look at me and said, 'You're sickening for something,' and hustled me straight to bed.

But by the following morning, I seemed normal again. Just very tired. And I didn't much like the look on my face in Dad's shaving mirror in the bathroom. All white and peaky. And I couldn't eat much breakfast.

'You'd better take it easy today,' said my mother. 'I'll get a deck-chair out for you, on the lawn. It's going to be another lovely day.'

But the book I tried to read didn't make any sense at all. There was only one thing I wanted. I could think of nothing else. By the time lunch was over, I had made myself enough of a nuisance to be allowed to go for a walk. Luckily my mother was a great believer in fresh air and exercise . . .

Valerie didn't muck about that day at all. She came swimming up out of the shadowed surface of the mirror as soon as I sat down at it. I thought how well she looked; she was smiling at me with that marvellous look on her face again.

'You were a naughty boy, yesterday. You did me a lot of good but yourself a lot of harm. We've got to look after you *properly*.'

'I still want to eat you.'

'Only a mouthful,' she said, and giggled, and touched me on the shoulder. I shuddered with delight. I realised I was sort of getting a taste for it; the cold.

But her hand was gone in a flash.

'Enough. Don't be greedy. Do you want to make yourself some tea?'

'No. I want to take you for a long walk. Along the pier.'

Even then, I had enough sense to want to get out of that cold, cold house.

'All right. I don't feel tired today. Thanks to you. Are you sure you feel well enough?'

'Try me.' I sounded cocky enough. But by the time we'd got to the High Light, my legs were already aching. I sat on a seat; and from a slight touch on my wrist, I knew she'd sat next to me. I looked at the infinite vastness of sky and sea and said to her (after a careful look round to make sure no one was watching), 'Isn't it marvellous? You feel you could take off and fly away for ever and ever . . .'

She was silent. Suddenly, she wasn't happy.

'I used to think the same,' she said. 'When I was ill, and fastened up in my bedroom, and could only look out of the window. I used to want to fly away then . . .'

'But now . . . ?' I knew I shouldn't have pressed her. I knew she wasn't wanting to talk about it. But we want to know, don't we? What's on the other side of everything? We want to know that more than anything. And people who've died should know, if anybody does . . .

'It's not like that at all,' she said, sadly. 'No blue sky and clouds. No angels with haloes. No God with a white beard . . .'

'What then?' I was hungry, avid. Like a wolf, like a shark. I *forced* her to it.

'There's just dark out there, Bob. Darkness and nothingness. The only light, only warm . . . is the

people who are still alive. They glow like . . . dim
suns. You want to warm yourself by being close to
them. But most of them, you find, are not very
nice. They won't give you any warm . . . they want
it all for themselves. They have so much of it, but
they're greedy for more. They try to snatch it from
each other. And most of them are full of rage like
volcanoes. I can't bear to be near them. It's much
worse than when you're alive . . . you feel it more,
somehow.'

'So . . . there's nowhere to go? No message . . .
from . . . ?'

'I only want to be close to you. Because you're the
only one who will give me warm.' Then she added,
'Please don't ask me again. Promise?'

'OK.' I suddenly felt guilty. 'Want a bit of warm
now?'

'No.' She said it quite sharply. 'I'm all right.
Only don't talk about it any more.'

'OK. But when I die, I'm going to explore even
the dark. There must be *something*. Perhaps you'd
better hang around and wait for me. Then we can
go together.'

She didn't answer.

And so we spent our time, in the hot afternoons;
while the fate of the world hung in the balance, far
to the south. We walked in her garden, where every
day the grass grew longer, and the vigorous weeds
covered the bare earth. Along the Bank Top, past
Nana's house, past the High Light, up to the Priory,
down along the pier. We never went down into the life

of the quay; too many people, too much rage and hate for her. I can hardly even remember meeting anyone on our walks, though we must have done, I suppose. I did not *want* to meet people; she did not want to meet people. We were enough in ourselves. We were all we wanted.

Back home, my Mam and Dad seemed to fade. I loved them dearly; but they were no longer important. I went through the motions of living, wearily. So wearily, my mother often threatened to take me to the doctor's. Then I had to look sharp and find something to do for her. It didn't matter what – dig over the garden for Dad, trim the privet, chop sticks, run up to the shops. Anything to give the impression of busy-ness, to stop her accusing me of 'moping'.

But all I wanted was to be with Valerie.

We were on the end of the pier again, when it happened. On another afternoon of sunlight. In memory, the sun always seemed to be shining, that summer.

There was no warning; no siren; no guns. The pier was empty, all its half-mile length, except for us. You never got anybody down there on weekdays, in the war. People were too busy on war-work. And frightened of being caught half a mile from any air-raid shelter, if a sneak raider dropped in.

As I said, no siren, no guns. Just the sudden sound of aircraft engines straining at full boost, and there they were, a Messerschmitt 110 and a fat Hurricane, chasing each other, not a thousand feet above the quiet sea. So low, you could see every detail. The twin-engined 110 was spotted in dabs of dark and light grey, with red spinners on its propellers. The Hurricane was the usual brown and green. Circling and circling, till they made you feel dizzy, and not a sound of machine-gun fire. They might have been alone in the world.

I knew all about what should have happened, for I was full of knowledge of aircraft, got from books. The Hurricane was just a shade faster, but much quicker at turning. It should have quickly got behind and below the enemy, closed the range and . . . bingo.

But the Messerschmitt had one trick up its sleeve. When it went into a steep climb or steep dive, its engines kept on going. When the Hurricane followed it, its engine would splutter, cough and die. And the German would gain a few hundred yards. Then the circling would start again.

It was enthralling; much better than any football match. My heart was in my mouth a hundred times. And yet, it was curiously abstract, as if they were two shiny insects. Like the time I had watched, in Dad's greenhouse, a wasp get caught in a spider's web. And the jewel-like spider trying to wrap the wasp deeper and deeper in its web, till it couldn't move. And the wasp's vigorous attempts to sting the spider, and the spider dodging.

It was *beautiful*; the curving, the diving. I didn't want it to stop. But the curious thing was that, unlike the time the Flying Pencil was shot down, I no longer wanted anyone to win. I was no longer shouting for our side. I was that far, now, from what I had once been; that far from life itself, the life of school, the competition to do somebody else down, the shouting and punching and kicking in the corridors, the need to half-kill Berry. I was already half out of the world.

It should have been a warning to me; but I was too enthralled to notice. Somehow, the character of the pilots came to me, through their flying. The German pilot was an old hand, wary, who knew every trick of surviving. The Hurricane bloke was new, over-keen, over-eager, making mistakes. I became, in my mind, first one, then the other. Oh, fly for ever; like the dancing midges over the lawn at sunset. . . .

The end came quickly. Suddenly, there were two more planes in the weaving pattern. With pointed wings. Spitfires . . .

The German's engines stopped. His shining circling prop-blades became sticks in the air. He glided on a straight track inland, waggling his wings violently. He was surrendering.

His surrender was accepted. The other three planes gathered around him, behind him, waggling their wings in turn. As they passed low overhead, I saw a Spitfire pilot pointing towards Acklington. And the German raised both hands from the steering-column and shrugged his shoulders, and re-started his engines. And so they vanished north. And I was glad no one had been killed.

I said as much to Valerie. But she didn't reply or touch me. She had gone; I had the pier to myself.

'Why didn't you stay?' I asked her the next day, as she swam up in the mirror.

'I was afraid,' she said.

'But they can't harm *you*!'

'I was afraid someone would get killed. It's awful, when someone dies. They disturb the air, as they pass.'

'Pass *where to*, Valerie?'

She didn't answer, and she was gone again from the mirror. And she didn't come back that day at all, though I waited till half past five, and made myself late for tea again. I was very miserable.

I nearly didn't go to her house at all the next day, I was that fed up.

Would it have been better or worse if I hadn't gone down?

Because I'd no sooner closed the gate behind me, silently, when there came a giggle from the bushes. More of a snort of laughter than a giggle, actually. And it wasn't Valerie. It was definitely male. And I had a very strong suspicion who it was, and my skin crept.

'Who's there?' I shouted. 'Who is it? Come on out. I know you're there.'

More snorts and giggles. I dashed wildly at the bushes, though I knew there were two or three of them there, standing giggling. I tore the branches apart.

And the hideous face of Berry leered out at me. And Whitaker and Burridge behind him.

'So this is where you get to on sunny afternoons?' said Berry. He had a nasty yellow spot on his left nostril. Just by being there, he made the world hideous.

'How did you know?' I screamed. 'How did you find out?' I knew I was going on like somebody demented, and they were loving every minute of it.

'Ve haff our spies everywhere,' said Berry, and they all laughed like sick cats. Then he said, 'We were at me aunty's. We followed you. Now ve haff discovered your secret life, sieg heil!'

'The Monktons are away on holiday,' I said. 'I come down to water the plants. My Dad asked me.'

'Liar,' said Burridge. 'We followed you down here yesterday. We saw you go in the house. You gotta key.'

'There are plants inside the house,' I said, trying to calm myself down and appear casual.

'C'mon then!' said Berry. 'Aren't you going to invite us in? For a cup of tea? I'll bet the Monktons have smashing cakes; and whole tins of chocolate biscuits off the Black Market. The Monktons have got pots of money. They won't miss a few.'

If they'd really been looking just for grub, I might have let them in. And given them cake to shut their mouths. But they didn't want just cake. They wanted trouble. Once they got into the house, anything might happen. . . .

'Get lost,' I shouted. 'I wouldn't let you in if you were the last people on earth. You've got manners like pigs.'

'Oooh,' said Berry. 'That's very *rude*. He's insulted us, lads. He'll have to pay for that.' They sidled into their usual attack positions, Berry still in front of me, and Whitaker and Burridge one to each side. They were going to hang on to my arms, while Berry

144

punched me in the gut as often as he liked. He never punched people in the face, because their Mams might notice.

I suppose I couldn't have stopped them, because I had suddenly realised I was much weaker than I usually was, and even at full strength, I would've found them more than a match for me. But as Whitaker grabbed my arm he said, 'And we'll get that key off him.'

And at that I went berserk. I forgot about the other two and punched Whitaker full in the face, which he wasn't expecting because usually kids didn't put up much of a fight with those three. Whitaker sat down hard on the path, blood streaming from his nose. Then they were really on to me.

But as I said I was berserk. I broke all the rules. I kicked. I bit Burridge on the arm. I gouged for eyes. I forgot everything but the urge to totally destroy them.

It seemed no time till they were on the far side of the shut gate, glaring at me with incredulous looks on their faces.

'He's bliddy bonkers,' said Burridge. 'Look, he *bit* me!'

'Frigging lunatic. Look – he's foaming at the mouth. Like Hitler. He ought to be put in *Morpeth*.'

Morpeth was the local lunatic asylum.

Their shocked pale faces said more. They said I was a pariah, in future. A sub-human. No longer part of the human race. A monster, fit only for baiting at a distance. I had broken every rule in the schoolboy code, and I knew it.

145

But I wasn't sorry. I was just glad they were on the far side of Valerie's gate, and wouldn't dare come through it again.

But it was Berry who stored up the most venom. He went all mock-reasonable and looked at me with mock-pity.

'There's something the matter with you, Bickerstaffe. You look *most* peculiar. I think something's gone wrong inside your head, Bickerstaffe. Maybe you're going to *die* or something.'

The he turned on his heel and walked away. And his two little jackals followed him.

And I somehow knew he would not keep his mouth shut. He was going to tell his parents.

I'd broken the schoolboy code. So why shouldn't he?

Chapter Fifteen

What I hadn't realised was that it would all happen so quickly. Two days later.

I was sitting at the dressing-table, and Valerie was resting her cold, cold hand ever so gently on my shoulder, when I heard the gate click.

I saw her face turn pale in the mirror.

'It's Daddy.'

I looked down, and Mr Monkton was hurrying up the path, with his head down. I could see long grey hairs on the top of his head, that I'd never noticed before. He looked ill, crumpled. I felt terrified. But more than terrified, I felt sorry. He was a good man really. I didn't want him to be hurt any more.

As I heard his key in the lock, I went slowly down the stairs to meet him. I wasn't going to lurk in the bedroom like a thief. I might have eaten some of his cake, but I wasn't a thief . . .

He looked up and saw me. He said, in an awed voice, 'What's happened to you, lad? You look like . . .' Then he stopped.

'Like what?'

He gave an uneasy little laugh. 'I was going to say you looked like a ghost. But it was just a trick of the light.' But from the way he kept staring at me, I knew he was lying. I knew I did look like a ghost.

'I've eaten some cake out of the tin,' I said. 'Valerie said I could have some.'

He put out a hand to the newel-post. I think he would have fallen if he hadn't. But he still kept staring at me. He didn't look like he thought I was insane. There were tears in his eyes, and a kind of mad hope.

'I've washed things up and tidied away,' I said. 'I haven't broken or stolen anything, honest.'

He sat down heavily on the second step of the stairs, and said, 'I never thought you were a thief, Bob Bickerstaffe. Or a vandal. I couldn't believe it when Mr Berry rang to tell me you were in our house. How did you get in?'

'I had Valerie's key. From that last walk. I found it in the lining of my jerkin, after she got bombed in the cemetery. It was a message from her. To come here.' I sat down on the stairs myself, a bit higher up. My legs wouldn't hold me up; and it was best to sit and talk where we couldn't see each other's faces.

He was silent a long time.

I said, 'She's here, you know. Upstairs in her bedroom.'

'You're mad, son,' he said gently. 'The shock's unhinged you. I'd better get you home to your Mam.' But I could tell from his voice that he didn't believe it. He *wanted* her to be here.

So I said, 'Come and see. She's been here all the time. She tried to make you understand. By knocking postcards off the mantelpiece.'

He said, incredulous, 'Postcards *did* keep falling off the mantelpiece . . .' Then he put his face in his hands, and again said nothing for a long time. I felt terrible. It was bad enough coping with Valerie, let alone him. He was her father. I could feel all the grief in him, and it was too big for me to cope with. I was sort of terrified of him and his silence. Then he got up at last and said, 'You'd better show me.' And I led him upstairs.

'I'm glad you've come,' I said. 'She hates being alone in the cold and dark. Have you come back for good?'

'I don't know,' he said. 'I don't know.' Then he added, shamefaced, staring at the empty room, and her nightdress on the bed, 'What do we do?'

'We sit and look in the mirror,' I said. 'She hates being looked at straight-on.'

He sat down so heavily on the little spindly chair that it creaked ominously; I thought it was going to break under his bulk. I fetched another chair, and sat next to him, and stared at our two faces in the mirror. How old he looked . . .

There was no sign of Valerie. I was dead scared she was going to muck about. I didn't want her Dad mucked about. It wouldn't be fair . . . So I was sharp with her.

'C'mon, Valerie. Don't mess about. Your Dad's tired . . .'

She swam up between our two faces in the mirror. She looked angry. Bloody angry. I couldn't make out why she was so angry.

'He won't be able to see me,' she said waspishly. 'He's *blind*. They're all blind.'

'Can you see her?' I asked her Dad gently.

'No,' he said. He sounded snarly too. If I wasn't careful, I was afraid they were both of them going to turn on me.

'I can't see a damned thing,' he said again. 'Not a damned thing.'

'See?' said Valerie. 'I told you. He can't hear me either. It's useless.'

I said desperately, 'Can't you do *something* to show him? He is your Dad. For God's sake, Valerie . . .'

'D'you think I'm a performing dog or something?' She was glaring at me with real hate now.

'Touch him,' I said. 'Touch him on the shoulder. Like you do with me.'

'Oh, all right.' She pressed him hard on the shoulder, on the epaulette of his military raincoat.

He shuddered, gasped, his mouth a little open as he still stared into the mirror.

'Now the other shoulder.'

'No.'

'I felt something,' said her Dad. 'I *felt* something. Cold.'

He looked like he was dying. He looked worse than me.

'I want to ask some questions,' he said.

'Will you answer questions?' I asked Valerie.

'I suppose so. I'm fed up with this. I wish he'd go *away*.' She looked diabolical. Trapped. Desperate.

'Ask . . . what she called her first doll.'

'Tuppence,' said Valerie. 'It had a stupid face, with spots of red in its cheeks.'

'Tuppence,' I told him. 'It had spots of red in its cheeks.'

150

'Oh, my God,' he moaned. Then, 'What was her pet name for Aunt Maggie?'

'Aggen,' said Valerie. 'I suppose it's too much to ask me how I am. How I *feel*.'

'Aggen,' I said, woodenly.

Again he moaned. I hoped he wasn't going to have a heart attack or anything. I couldn't cope as it was.

'Ask her . . . what I used to call the stairs, when she was a baby.'

'Up the little wooden hill to Bedfordshire. And that's the last question I'm answering.'

'She *is* here,' said Mr Monkton. After a long pause, he said, 'Will you leave us together for a bit, Bob?'

I staggered outside. I was glad to go. I nearly fell downstairs, I was so weak. I just sat on the hall chair. I could hear him talking upstairs, but I couldn't make out what he was saying. I didn't want to know. It was sacred. It was terrible.

At last he came down, holding the handrail all the way.

'You mustn't come here any more, Bob,' he said.

I looked at him in agony. 'Don't you *believe* me?'

'I do believe you. That's why you mustn't come here any more.'

'But *why*?'

'She shouldn't be here, Bob. It's against all . . .' He couldn't bring himself to say what it was all against. But I knew his word was final.

'But she'll be so *lonely*. In the cold and dark . . .'

'It's my problem now, Bob. She's my daughter. I

151

have to take the responsibility. You've got your life to lead . . .'

'But she *needs* me!'

'She needs you too much. She's half-killed you, son. You look like you can hardly walk.'

I just felt there was no point in arguing with him. I didn't have any strength left to argue.

'Can I say goodbye to her?'

'I don't think you should . . .'

'But I can't just walk out on her . . .'

'I'll see you home. I owe that much to your Dad.'

'*Please* let me say goodbye.'

He took a firm grip on my arm; like a policeman arresting somebody. Grown-ups are very strong, even when they're tired to death.

But still I squawked on, about wanting to say goodbye.

Until something came hurtling down the stairs, and broke on the coloured tiles at the bottom. A tiny square of glass, scattered out of its frame in a hundred glinting pieces. I bent to look.

It was a photograph of her mother.

I let him lead me away, then. He took me home, and my mother put me to bed. I was in a whirling daze, but I remember their voices rumbled on and on in the kitchen, till I fell asleep.

Chapter Sixteen

I never knew what time it was. But one moment I was fast asleep, and the next I was wide awake. I was lying facing the wall, and I just knew . . .

I lay with a mounting sense of excitement. She was coming, she was coming. Searching, searching for me. I felt her fear of the dark; of the gusts of rage and the disturbed dreams that rose from every house of the sleeping town. Her distaste for all the sordidness of life, the rumpled piles of clothes on the ends of the beds, the smelly socks and quarrels of couples lying awake unable to sleep. The whole mess of the world, where people lived cramped up in warrens like rabbits. She was searching, trembling, coming. I sensed her get lost; I sensed her confidence give out. And yet she kept on coming, searching for *me*.

And then a rush of gladness. She was near; she was very near.

I half sat up in bed. And then she was standing poised on the windowsill of my bedroom. Beautiful as she had never been beautiful before. Tall, stately, the red hair streaming down her nightdress, on each side of her long pale face.

She smiled. She said, 'I found you. I was so frightened, but I found you. I didn't think I could

153

manage it. I've never come so far before without you. Don't you think I'm brave?'

She moved closer, right by my bed. She looked at me with a solemn glowing love. There was high colour in her cheeks.

'Love *is* stronger than the grave,' she said. 'But I'm cold, cold. Aren't you going to let me in? Now I've come so far? For *you.*'

I think I held out my arms, and she came into them. The coldness of her still took my breath away. Like the coldness of a wave of the sea. But I was used to it now. It wasn't pain any more. It was ecstasy. It was the fresh beauty of a new morning fall of snow, before the milkman's horse tramples in it, and ruins it with a melting heap of horse-dung. It was the beauty of Mount Everest, and the endless cleanness of the sea.

She whispered in my ear, 'They tried to separate us. They're jealous of us. My father is *terribly* jealous. He just shouts at me all the time now. He won't leave me alone. I think he hates me.'

Later, I think she whispered, 'I only want you.'

And later still, 'Soon, they won't be able to separate us any more.'

I suppose you might say it was a dream . . .

Then suddenly it was morning, and my mother was shaking my shoulder and shouting at me, and I could hardly see out of my eyes for some grey sticky curtain, and I just wanted to sleep and sleep, until Valerie came again.

The next time I was shaken awake, the doctor was there. He was a good bloke, Dr Armstrong.

One of the best. Usually he only came to see my father, when my father had the flu. He wasn't the toffee-nosed sort like most doctors. After he'd diagnosed what was wrong, and written a prescription, he'd sit by Dad's bedside and accept a cup of tea, and talk. He was a fascinating talker; he'd been in the Indian Army, and had some rare tales of fakirs with their beds of nails and Indian Rope Tricks, so that I would first listen at Dad's bedroom door, and then find some excuse for going in and sitting on the bed.

But this morning I just wished he'd go away and leave me in peace. Instead, he made me sit up, and rolled up my pyjama-top, and held the cold end of his stethoscope against my back, and asked me to say 'Ninety-nine' and breathe deep.

He tapped my ribs with his fingers, so I sounded like a drum. Then asked my Mam how I was eating, and about my bowels being moved. I was listening to it all, in a shut-eyed cunning sort of way. He sounded baffled, and cross because he was baffled, and yet . . . a bit scared underneath.

Then they went out into the hall, and closed the bedroom door so I couldn't hear. Which was a waste of time, because I have very sharp ears.

'Afraid it's pneumonia . . . can't understand it, this weather. It's just not pneumonia weather. If he'd got himself soaked to the skin, and walked home through a blizzard now . . . but we're practically in the middle of a heat-wave, and it's not rained for weeks. And he seems to have no will to fight it. I see it in very old people, this wanting to slip away quietly. But not in a

155

young lad with all his life before him. It doesn't make *sense.*'

My mother's worried murmuring. Then the doctor's voice sharp again. 'I'm afraid it's hospital for him. I'll ring up for a bed in Preston Hospital . . . have to be men's medical, I'm afraid, but beggars can't be choosers. Will you have him ready by two o'clock? We can't afford to take any risks. I don't want to lose him.'

Even in my grey fuddle, I saw what Dr Armstrong meant by the men's medical ward.

The last time, with my ears, I had been in men's surgical. That had been full of middle-aged blokes, miners getting over hernia ops and air-raid casualties. Lots of crude laughs and attempts to chat up the pretty nurses, and a bit of bum-pinching while they were making the beds. Blokes would hop across to your bed like crippled chimpanzees and offer to lend you their copy of the *Daily Mirror* with Jane half-naked as usual; or tell you all about their racing-pigeons.

But men's surgical was the real no-hopers. Blokes so grey in the face they made the bed sheets look bright pink. Blokes who just lay all day and stared at the ceiling, like bits of flotsam cast up on the beach. And cough, cough, cough, echoing up and down the length of the endless long ward.

I lay in the dark now and listened to the symphony of breathing, coughing and wheezes. It sort of caught at my mind the way a dripping tap does. I found myself straining my ears to make sure the bloke in the next bed but four hadn't suddenly snuffed it. Every so often, I raised my head to look along the row of beds to where the night-sister sat at her desk reading. She seemed so far away, like at the end of a telescope. But she had nice legs and a pretty face; she was like a single flower on a burnt-out bomb-site. Whenever she passed, I couldn't take my eyes off her.

She was a bit like Valerie, with her long straight nose and clean-chiselled lips. But her big eyes were sharp blue, not grey-green. . . .

I closed my eyes and tried to close my ears, and thought of cleaner things. Of the sea; great waves breaking on the beach in the early morning, and the taste of salt on your lips, and nobody on the beach but you and a big wet black dog that wanted you to throw a stick in the sea for it. Of the mountains of the Lake District where we'd spent our last holiday; just the sunlit silence, and the odd sheep baa-ing. I thought of Spitfires zooming up through great canyons of cloud, free, free. And I thought of Valerie, who could never venture in here. I was glad, in a miserable way. I didn't want her seeing all this. She was better off out of it.

And then I heard her giggle. Like she was very pleased with herself, and it was the funniest thing in the world.

I opened my eyes, and there she was in this dreadful place. All love. All beauty. Against all hope, she had found me.

* * *

157

The next morning, I was half-wakened out of muzzy dreams by my bed being moved on its squeaky wheels. By the time I had got my eyes open, and taken stock of my surroundings, I was in a little room by myself. The sun was shining in through a big window. There was a patch of sunlight on my bed, and I moved my hand into it. The patch of sunlight was beautifully warm; the only lovely thing in that whole hospital. All day, I kept waking up and seeing that patch of sun, and moving my hand into it. It was all I did. It was very peaceful, dozing and waking, dozing and waking.

That night, I awakened to a shock. The light was still on, over my bed, and my father was sitting by my bed. He looked very tired, but was reading the *Shields Evening News*. I liked the way he had his reading-specs perched on the end of his nose; it reminded me of home; he looked so peaceful I didn't disturb him.

But the odd thing was that, in the dark corner, behind my father, Mr Monkton was sitting too. He wasn't reading. He was . . . waiting. I studied his face in the shadow. He looked weary, but he looked angry too, somehow. He sat so still, yet he looked so angry. I just hoped he wasn't angry with me; but I knew by then that I was too ill for anyone to be angry with, so I fell asleep again.

And then in the morning, the nurse came to wash me. And I realised that Valerie hadn't come.

The next night, when I wakened, my Dad and Mr Monkton were there again. Mr Monkton looked wearier than ever; but he was still very watchful; even a bit jumpy. His eyes kept roving into the corners

158

of the room, like he was on sentry-duty. I felt safe, somehow, because he was there, and slept again.

The following morning, the doctor came and pulled me about and pronounced that some crisis had passed. He ordered me some porridge for breakfast. It tasted bloody awful, but I got it all down, because I was hungry.

I realised that Valerie hadn't come again.

That day too I spent moving my hand in the patch of sunlight on the bed. Till I got bored and read the *Shields Evening News* my Dad had left for me. I even had one bit of a laugh, because in the court reports, one William Dominic Talbot Welsh had been up in court for being drunk and disorderly for the two hundred and fourteenth time. He was a great favourite of mine, at least in the pages of the *Evening News*. Hitlers might come, and Hitlers might go; we might win or lose the Battle of Britain, but William Dominic Talbot Welsh would go on for ever.

Towards teatime, they took me home. I was glad to see our dog, and he was glad to see me. But I felt as weak as a kitten, still, and was glad to get to bed.

That night, when I awakened, the light was still on in my bedroom, and Mr Monkton was sitting by my bed again. If it had seemed odd to have him in hospital, it seemed even odder to have him here.

He smiled a weary smile at me, and said, 'You're awake.'

And I said, 'What're you doing here.'

And he said, 'Making sure our Valerie doesn't do you any more harm.'

I gaped at him. 'You know?'

'I guessed. I'm not a total fool. I raised our Valerie. I know her. She was always one for getting what she wanted.'

'You can't blame her,' I said. 'She's scared of the cold and dark. She just wants to go on . . . being.'

'And it doesn't matter who else suffers,' he said. Bitterly. 'She thinks the rules don't apply to her. She thinks she's not the same as everybody else. She's a bit like her mother, that way. Only worse. Eat you body and soul.'

'You've *seen* her?'

'Oh, aye, I've seen her. Once you convinced me she was there, I saw her soon enough. And she's taken to knocking things off shelves. But if she thinks she can get her way with me, she's got another thing coming. I'll stop her little games, if it's the last thing I do.'

'Does her mother know . . . ?'

'Her mother's still in the West Country. Where she'll stay, till this business is sorted out. I'm not having our Valerie doing harm to another man's bairn.'

'She doesn't *mean* any harm.'

'She's taking what's not hers. Your life.'

'She wants me to go with her. She's scared.'

He stared at me a long time; I couldn't read the expression on his face. Then he said, 'You're too good for this bloody world, son.' The funny thing was, the way he said it, it didn't sound like any kind of compliment. Then he said, in a gentler voice, 'You have to give people what they need; not what they

160

want. Give in to what they want, and they'll have the skin off your body for making boots. *And* complain about the quality.'

'What you going to do with her?'

'If I can keep her off you, she'll *have* to go, sooner or later. But I'd rather she went willing. I've got to live wi' meself after. I don't like her being out there in the dark and cold any more than you do.'

'What've you told me Dad?'

'Enough. He knows you were dyin'. An' now he knows you're not. He trusts me.'

I drifted off to sleep again.

The following morning, I was well enough to get up and sit in a chair in the sitting-room, listening to the radio. The sun still shone, and the world seemed a nice place again. Nothing grand, mind. Just the dog, and sausage and chips for lunch, and my mother doing the ironing and humming to herself and giving me the odd little smile to say she was glad I was better. She didn't seem inclined to speak about Valerie; and neither did I. But once she said, 'You've got your whole life before you.'

And I said, 'That's what worries me.' But I gave her a grin to prove I was only joking.

I think Mr Monkton stayed two more nights with me. That seemed to be enough. The third morning I felt so good I went out into the garden to do a bit of weeding for Dad. The sun was on my back, and the smell of the disturbed soil went up my nose. Sun and soil have a funny effect on me. They're so much *there*, they make the things in your mind seem thin and ghostly. It wasn't that I stopped loving Valerie;

she just sort of faded away in the air, like the smoke from Mr Hunnicutt's bonfire next door. I began to think about starting school again, and wondering where my rugby boots had got to, over the summer, and whether they'd still fit me.

That night, over tea, my Dad said, 'I don't like to ask you this, and you can say no. But George Monkton wants a favour off you.'

Suddenly, out of nowhere, my heart was racing.

'Valerie?'

'He's having a bad time. He showed me the house. It's half-wrecked wi' her goings-on. He looks like he hasn't slept for a month. He's a strong feller, but even he's got limits.'

'OK,' I said. 'What does he want me to do?'

'He's done a lot for you,' said my father. 'I reckon he saved your life . . .' He always goes on coaxing me, even after I've said yes. It's one of the few ways he's always irritated me.

'OK, OK, OK,' I said, with a sudden burst of anger. 'Just tell me what he wants, and I'll do it.'

'He wants you to go down and reason with her, one last time. I think he's got some vicar going down an' all. Tomorrow afternoon. I'll come with you, if you like.'

'It's OK,' I said quickly. 'I'll go on me own. I'm a big boy now.'

'By God,' said my father. 'Ye could have fooled me.' He made a joke of it, but I could tell he was worried.

* * *

I went through that gate for the last time. It still creaked in the same way, only worse.

The garden was terribly overgrown by then; weeds sprouting everywhere. It seemed so sad; it had been so lovely, once. It seemed like years ago. I felt angry. With Hitler? With Valerie?

One of the panes of glass in the front door was broken. Hitler? Valerie? Burglars?

Mr Monkton opened the door. His hair was all messed up, and the collar of his shirt was black round the top. He looked like he'd slept in his clothes. But he still took my hand firmly, and said, 'Thanks for coming.'

He was a good bloke. I suddenly felt angry with Valerie for the first time; knowing she'd done this to him. Suddenly, she did seem like a thief and a robber.

He took me into the sitting-room. There was a vicar sitting there, dressed all in black and looking solemn. An old man with silver hair. He took my hand in both of his large ones and said, 'How are you, my boy?' in a deep booming pretendy voice. I didn't think he was going to cut much ice with Valerie. He wasn't cutting much ice with me.

We all sat down again, and Mr Monkton and I looked at him.

'Perhaps we might start with prayer,' he said.

He started. The trouble was, he didn't seem able to stop. He was the sort who told God what God already knew. I didn't feel he was cutting much ice with God, either.

There was a giggle, just behind me. A teasing

icy hand ran its fingers lightly up my spine. Valerie's little way of letting me know she was there. Nobody else seemed to have noticed. It really was very funny, the vicar booming on, and not noticing, and Valerie playing tricks and giggling. I nearly sniggered out loud in the middle of the prayers.

Then I realised that was what she wanted. She wanted to split me off from the others; she wanted me to join in playing tricks on them. I opened my eyes.

And saw Mr Monkton's poor ravaged face.

That settled it. I said, in a flash of anger, 'She's here. She's tickling me, trying to get me to laugh at the prayers.'

'*Traitor!*' Valerie really spat it out. She was glaring at me now, from the shadows by the door. 'You're on their side. You've let them turn you against me. I thought you said you loved me.'

'It's for your own good,' I said back.

'For your own good,' she mocked me. 'For your own good. That's what they've always said. It was never for *my* good. It was for *theirs*. Always. I'm being a nuisance. I was always a nuisance, from the day I was born. Poor little sickly thing.'

The vicar and Mr Monkton were both staring at me, mouths wide open. It was obvious they hadn't seen or heard a thing. I was on my own with Valerie again.

'Look, be reasonable,' I said.

'Why should I be reasonable? Is life reasonable? Why should you be alive when I'm dead? What have I done to deserve to be dead? You'll probably live to be ninety. Why? *Why?* Tell me, *why?* If you're so *clever . . .*'

We were going hammer and tongs. The vicar and Mr Monkton might as well not have been there. I was blind and deaf to them.

But I was a blitz child too. A Battle of Britain child. An old hand at survival, now. Much too cunning at survival not to hear, far away and very faint, borne on the warm breeze through the half-drawn curtains of the window, the air-raid siren sounding at Sunderland, five miles down the coast. Even when I was all concerned with her, my ears heard, and my stomach tightened at the sound of the siren. Like it always did. And while I still yelled at her, my ears were cocked for other sounds that spelt earthly danger.

Two sharp cracks, that echoed round the whole sky.

Heavy ack-ack, out to sea.

Then our own siren went.

The vicar shuffled uncomfortably in his chair. 'Perhaps we ought to retire . . .'

'Shelter's in the garden, just outside the back door,' said George Monkton. He gestured with his hand, but made no attempt to move. His eyes were on my face . . .

'Well, what have you got to say for yourself?' shouted Valerie. Real little prima donna; couldn't bear to be neglected even for an air-raid.

Through the open window came the heavy thrumming of engines. Jerry planes. Unsynchronised engines, going hoom-hoom-hoom, whereas ours made a steady drone. Going to be a big raid.

The vicar's nerve broke, and he fled. We heard his footsteps running down the hall to the back door and safety.

'Well?' said Valerie.

Five tremendous bangs overhead. A whistling in the air, a kind of fluttering in the air. Falling shrapnel rattled on the house roof.

'Run away to the shelter, little boy,' said Valerie. 'Because if they kill you, I've *got* you! For *good!*'

'If they kill me,' I shouted, 'then I'll go to the place I'm supposed to go to. And I'll take you with me, as well. So you'll stop tormenting your Dad.'

'How heroic of you. I didn't know you were so fond of my father. What's he ever done for you?'

'He's a bloody good bloke . . .'

I suppose we were having a row as only lovers can. Lost in rage at each other; nobody in the world but each other.

Except I heard a distant mournful wail, getting slowly louder and louder. A badly damaged plane, plunging to earth, getting nearer and nearer. Any other time, I'd have run for the shelter like a frightened rabbit. But I wouldn't give her that satisfaction. I glared at her face; her face; her face.

Louder the wail, louder. Torn aluminium ripping the air apart, pilot wrestling hopelessly with the controls, tons of bombs, hundreds of gallons of aviation spirit, the whole thing a bomb bigger than any bomb that had ever been dropped. Death was coming, and coming fast, straight at us. It was so loud now it could only be coming for us. It was the one that had our number on it, as my Dad used to say.

Her face lit up with a terrible look of triumph. But I knew that, once dead, I'd be stronger than she was. I'd soon show her who was boss. I'd make her sorry for all she'd done. She'd cry, then she'd do what *I* said. And that would be *very* satisfying; she'd be mine, to do what I liked with.

But another part of me cried out that I'd hardly *begun*. My exams, the university, the rugby team, Mam, Dad, Nana, the dog, they couldn't all just *stop* . . .

But the journey in the dark with her. Together. Exciting. What would we find? *Together*?

The noise of screeching and tearing in the air filled my ears, filled my head. I couldn't have heard her Dad's voice now. I couldn't have heard my own even. But hers I heard.

'C'mon,' she said, coaxing, holding out a hand. 'It's *easy*. Dying's the easiest thing in the world . . .'

There was no sound of an explosion. I just saw the glass of the windows sleet across the room, into the glass of the huge mirror over the mantelpiece. Felt myself picked up like a baby, and hurled into a corner. Then, before I could open my eyes, felt myself picked up again, and sucked towards the broken window. Fell over an upturned chair, that held me partly upright.

So that I saw.

Not just Valerie; but another figure in the room with Mr Monkton and me. A tall thin figure with leather tight round his head, and goggles up on his forehead, and a mass of harness meeting in the middle of a grey tunic. For a moment, he stared at us in uncomprehending amazement. The uncomprehending amazement on the face of the newly dead (for I have seen it since).

Then his glance switched from me to Valerie.

He frowned, as if something was wrong. Then he made an urgent commanding gesture towards her.

'*Raus*! *Raus*!'

A gesture that comprehended the whole sky, the whole earth. An *outwards* gesture. She shrank away from him.

Then he held out a hand to her; a hand inside a sheepskin gauntlet, half blown away.

'Komm!' he shouted. '*Komm*!' A voice that knew duty, and obeyed. And yet perhaps it had softened a little. Perhaps he even smiled at her.

Certainly she smiled back at him. I could almost call it a flirty smile. It's imprinted on my mind for ever; the last glimpse I had of her.

And then they were both gone, and the room was just full of swirling plaster-dust, and Mr Monkton was staggering towards me, coughing up his whole lungs, it seemed, and with a streak of dark red blood flowing down his cheek.

'You all right, son?' He managed to get it out somehow.

'Did you see?' I shouted. 'Did you *see*?'

He shook his head as if to clear it. 'I saw . . . something.'

'She's gone. She's *gone*.'

'Aye,' he said. 'I think she has. For good.' Then his mind seemed to change gear. 'Blast can do funny things. And shock. You must be in shock, son. I must make you some hot sweet tea . . . if I can find the kitchen any more.'

But it wasn't towards the kitchen that we turned. It was towards the yellow light and heat streaming in through the swirling dust; from the window, the shattered window.

The whole garden seemed to be on fire. Streams of fire flowed down the terraces towards the river. With the air shimmering over them. And, in the midst of the shimmering, a grey tailfin, a dark-grey tailfin, with a black swastika painted on it.

'Junkers 88,' I said, automatically. Then the skin of the tail stripped away like tissue-paper in the mass of flame, leaving just a blackened skeleton. And the blackened skeleton began to crumble in its turn.

Then the heat on our faces grew unbearable. Three yards away, in the garden, an ornamental bush, green leaves with yellow spots, burst into flame. All the long grass of the lawn was curling up like hay, and then going black and then glowing like fireworks.

'Out, son,' yelled Mr Monkton. 'Run for your life.'

We ran down the still-cool hall to the back door, and hauled the vicar out of the shelter and got as far away as possible, quickly.

Then we turned, in the clean air of the Bank Top, and looked back, and watched his half-shattered house take fire.

'Look at those parachutes coming down,' said the vicar.

We looked. Beyond the burning, three parachutes

169

were dropping into the estuary of the Tyne, between the piers.

'The rest of his crew,' said Mr Monkton. 'He must have stayed with his plane, to give them a chance to get out. He must have been the pilot.'

We just went on standing, watching the house burn.

'Just as well,' he said. 'I could never have borne to live there again.'

'She's gone,' I said.

'Aye, she's gone. I feel it. I hope that German feller looks after her.'

'He looked after his crew . . .'

Then I said, 'I shall miss her.' There were tears in my eyes. Or was it the smoke of the burning?

'Aye, so shall I. But she'll be all right, where she's gone.' The tears were rolling down his cheeks as well. Somehow, it was all right to cry.

He gripped my hand, with a grip like a vice. 'I owe you, son. I owe you more than . . . I shan't forget. If there's ever anything you need . . .'

The vicar turned away, embarrassed. I don't know how long we'd have stood there, gripping both hands with both hands. Looking each other in the face, as the tears streamed down. But the vicar called out, 'Here come the wardens.'

And we told the wardens what we could.